THE AINSWICK ORANGE

SUSAN ALEXANDER

MINERVA

Susan Alexander

Text copyright © 2013

Susan Alexander

All rights reserved.

All characters in this publication are fictional. Any resemblance to persons living or dead is purely coincidental.

Also by the author

The Snowdrop Mysteries:
The Snowdrop Crusade
A Remittance Man
The Heracles Project
St Margaret's
Hereford Crescent
Wolcum Yole
Gnat
And Only Man is Vile

A Woman's Book of Rules

The Ainswick Orange

To Ernest

Galanthophile extraordinaire

SUSAN ALEXANDER

Chapter One. Cotswold Beauty

A slim, graceful flower whose inner segments display an elongated "X," 'Cotswold Beauty' is a clone selected by Phil Cornish from the Gloucestershire garden of E.B. Anderson at Lower Slaughter and named by Daphne Chapell.

'Cotswold Beauty' is a complex hybrid whose ancestors are likely G. gracilis and G. plicatus. 'Cotswold Beauty' often produces two and sometimes even three scapes. Its outer segments are long and elegant and its inner segments flare at the apex. It blooms in early mid-season.

"Well, it seemed like a good idea at the time," Maggie thought to herself as she pushed back her chair from the dining table she was using as a desk and headed to the kitchen for some coffee. She was careful not to trip on the uneven flagstone floor and ducked as she went through the doorway, built during a period when people were shorter. Shorter than her five feet, eleven inches, anyhow.

Uh oh. The kitchen seemed unusually cold, even for February. She walked over to the Aga and held out her hands. Oh dear. It was barely radiating any heat. That wasn't good. She bent down to peer at the gauge. The indicator which should have been squarely between the red and black bars was hovering over the black.

Maggie knew that meant the giant, cream-enamelled, cast iron beast of a cooker was not hot enough. Now what was it that Anne had told her to do when this happened? Darned if she could remember.

First she'd start the coffee. Then she'd call Anne. Thankfully she had brought her own coffee maker with her from Oxford. She did the fill-the-container-with-water thing and then the filter-and-coffee-grounds thing and pushed the On button. At least this machine was working.

Maggie pulled her mobile from her pocket and began to call Anne, then remembered she had no reception in the kitchen. She would need to go into the sitting room to get a strong-enough signal.

A lesser woman might blame her friend at this point.

"But I am not a lesser woman," Maggie thought as she pulled herself to her full height, while being careful to avoid the wood beams in the low ceiling that she had at first found so charming.

After all, it was hardly Anne's fault that Maggie had long had a fantasy about living in an English country cottage.

It was hardly Anne's fault that she just happened to know a woman who was off to Australia for six months where her daughter was giving birth to a first grandchild and welcomed the idea of a housesitter.

And it was hardly Anne's fault that, with only a few months to go before her publisher's deadline, Maggie had succumbed to a full-blown case of writer's block.

Maggie, known in academic circles as Professor Margaret Spence Eliot, Appleton Fellow of Global Issues at Merrion College, Oxford, was enjoying a sabbatical year and was supposed to be writing a book on her areas of expertise, which were immigration and cultural integration. She had finished all her research the previous autumn and had been preparing to begin writing, when the Christmas holiday season had arrived and she had become... distracted.

THE AINSWICK ORANGE

Perhaps it was because it was the first anniversary of her father's death, back in her native Boston. Perhaps it was a delayed mid-life crisis. Whatever it was, after two weeks of sitting in front of her laptop with screen blank except for a title page, she had seen Anne at a faculty Christmas party and confessed her problem.

Anne Brooks was the wife of a colleague, Laurence, who ran the Institute for Global Development at the University. Anne had been exceptionally helpful when Maggie had first arrived from Boston eight years before and they had become friends.

Anne had been sympathetic and said that she had supported Laurence through more than one dry spell and that perhaps she had a solution. Maybe what Maggie needed was a change of scene. Someplace quiet where she could work without the distractions of her life in Oxford. And Anne had known just the place.

So here Maggie was, in a quaint little cottage in the Cotswolds, in a picturesque village, no, a hamlet, consisting of a dozen other dwellings, a church and a pub. It was certainly a distraction-free environment and Maggie had been charmed when she had first arrived. Now, however, more than a month later, with her research neatly stacked in piles on the dining room sideboard, but no further advanced on her book, she was beginning to feel panic.

She called Anne, got her voice mail and left a message. "Hi, Anne. It's Maggie. Would you please give me a call when it's convenient? It's about the Aga. Again."

Maggie heard the sound like a death rattle that the coffee machine made when the coffee was ready. She was about to return to the kitchen, when Bear stalked in.

Bear was Maggie's cat and another of Anne's good deeds. On the board of the local animal rescue league and a magnet for abandoned kittens, Anne had turned up on Maggie's doorstep with one of her orphans on a day when Maggie was recovering from a relationship break up.

What had been presented to Maggie as a colleague's separation-in-the-process-of-divorce had turned out to be a wife's-visiting-her-sister-in-Canada while the latter went through chemotherapy. Maggie was furious, then depressed. Anne was certain the kitten she had brought in a wicker basket was just what Maggie needed to cheer her up.

With a given name of Ursula, the kitten had become Ursa, after Ursa Major, the bear constellation, as she grew into an eighteen-pound beast. From that Ursa became, simply, Bear. Bear was a tortoiseshell and the genetic mutation which gave her a variegated coat of black, brown, marmalade and cream also affected her behaviour.

Anne had warned Maggie that tortoiseshells were "special" and the veterinarian had characterised Bear as "easily stressed." As Maggie watched the cat, with her back end going in not quite the same direction as her front, she thought of the Stegosaurus, whom she had heard required a second brain in its tail to navigate its giant body. Maybe that was what Bear needed.

Maggie put out her hand to pat Bear on the head, but the cat froze, then loped off upstairs. Bear had not yet fully adjusted to her new environment.

"That's okay, Bear," said Maggie to the retreating cat.

Her mobile sounded. It was Anne, calling back.

"Hi, Anne. Thanks for returning my call. I'm afraid it's the Aga."

"No problem, Maggie. Listen. I'm ten minutes away. How about I come by and give what you academics like to call a lecture demonstration. I won't be interrupting your work, will I?"

"If only," said Maggie.

"Oh dear. Well, see you in a bit, then."

"Thanks. I just made some fresh coffee."

"Perfect."

Ten minutes later, Maggie heard the lion's head knocker on the front door and opened it to her friend. Pretty and slim, with brown eyes and short hair expertly highlighted in a half-dozen shades of honey, Anne had raised three sons and been a model academic wife. She lived nearby in a beautifully kept Georgian house, was active in her church and a range of local community groups and was a respected cook and gardener.

"Thanks for coming, Anne. I'm hopeless, I'm afraid. The Aga, it's gone cold."

"My pleasure, Maggie. I was nearby and you were on my way. Let's go and take a look."

The women went into the kitchen.

"See, you turn this clockwise to turn up the heat." Anne had opened one of the doors and was turning a small knob.

"Turn it clockwise," Maggie repeated.

"There," Anne closed the door. "It's really simple, once you get used to it."

"Right," said Maggie, a more polite version of the "Yeah, right," she was thinking to herself.

"Coffee?"

"Please."

Maggie got out two mugs, poured coffee and put out milk and sugar. The women sat down at a small kitchen table. Maggie could feel that the Aga was warmer already.

Anne looked at her friend. "So, how's it going?"

Maggie sighed. "It's not."

"Oh dear."

"I don't know what's wrong with me. I can't get motivated. I surf the internet. I do housework. I make soup. I read so much news I must know more about current affairs than anyone else in Britain. Anything but write. I sit down to write and I become paralysed."

"Sounds bad," Anne sympathised.

"When I'm in the shower, the words just flow into my head. Then I come down and sit in front of the screen and I've gone blank again. What's wrong with me?"

Anne gave a sympathetic cluck.

"I've written books before. Journal articles. Textbooks. Newspaper columns. I've never had a problem. Do you think it's something to do with having gone through the menopause?"

Anne laughed and shook her head. "No. Or I hope not. If it is, we're both doomed."

She took a sip of coffee. "Maggie, when was the last time you took a break? A real break? Did something not related to your work?"

"Well, I go to London occasionally for a weekend. Paris maybe once a year. Conferences here and there."

"Conferences are work."

"What, do you think I need a vacation?"

"It's a theory."

"Hmm."

"Anyway, I have a proposition."

"Yes?" Maggie sounded dubious.

"Maud Wiggins and I had signed up for a special programme this weekend, but last night, well, gall stones. Maud is having her gall bladder out tomorrow."

Both women paused and considered the frailties of aging flesh. Maggie mentally knocked on wood.

"So Maud's out, but her place is all paid for. Accommodation. Meals. The lot. Unrefundable. And it was hard to get in. We've been booked for weeks."

"Too bad," said Maggie sympathetically.

"So what I'm thinking… Why don't you come with me?"

"Me? Um, what's this programme exactly?"

"It's a galanthophile weekend."

"Galantho-what?"

"Galanthophile."

"Er, Anne. I'm not sure I..." Maggie looked embarrassed.

Anne laughed. "Oh, you think it's something sexual? No, no, no. It's from Galanthus. The botanical name for snowdrops. A galanthophile is someone who loves snowdrops. Collects them. Certainly you've seen the articles in the media, if you've been following the news."

Maggie vaguely remembered something. Some craze. Like with tulips.

"You know what snowdrops are, don't you?"

"Those small white flowers?"

"They're all over the Cotswolds at this time of year. I expect there are even some in the garden here."

Maggie tried to recall if she had seen any.

"Anyhow, Rochford Manor has one of the world's finest snowdrop gardens. Lord and Lady Ainswick—the viscount and his wife—have organised a long weekend at the estate. Lectures, workshops, garden tours, a dinner with an auction including some of their rarer specimens. They've limited it to only a dozen people. Including us."

"Us?" echoed Maggie.

"Oh come on, Maggie. It will be fun. Aren't you the one who says you need to learn new things to keep your brain in shape?"

"Guilty as charged."

"And we've rooms at the Rochford Inn. It's an eighteenth century coaching house that's been renovated. Good food, locally sourced. Decent wine list."

"Oh Anne, I don't know…"

"What? You think you're going to get up tomorrow and suddenly the dam will burst? The words will flow? Really. Take a break. It couldn't hurt and it might help. It will be fun. You remember. Fun? And I'd be grateful. I would prefer not to go all on my own."

Anne had Maggie there. She owed her.

"All right." Maggie tried to sound more enthused than resigned.

"Tell me what I've just agreed to."

Anne reached into her handbag and pulled out some papers. It was a print-out of the weekend's schedule.

"I'll pick you up tomorrow at 8:30 and we'll drive over. The programme starts at 9:30 with an introductory lecture, followed by a tour of the Rochford Manor garden. Lunch is at the inn. In the afternoon there are more lectures and a tour of a neighbouring garden. Then back to the inn and dinner with the group.

"We have the traditional full English breakfast at the inn the next morning, then more study. Cocktails and a dinner at Rochford Manor on Saturday night, followed by the snowdrop auction. I guess they hope if we've had enough to drink, it will stimulate the bidding.

"On Sunday, another full English breakfast at the inn, then a final lecture, lunch, a workshop on chipping and twin scaling, which is how you get many snowdrop plants out of one bulb, tea and we're off. You'll be back in time for your

Sunday night supper and ready to hit the keyboard early on Monday."

Maggie had to smile at her friend's enthusiasm.

"Do you know anyone else who is going?" she asked.

"Just Derek Fiske and Damien Hawking. They're garden designers who also have a small garden centre outside of Burford where I go."

Maggie frowned. "What should I wear? I don't have Wellies. Or a Barbour. And dinner with a viscount?"

Anne examined her friend in her wool slacks, cashmere turtleneck and loafers.

"What you're wearing now is fine. Sturdier shoes or some boots for the gardens. A warm jacket, although the weather is supposed to be nice. Sunny and in the high forties. We're lucky. Last February we had snow."

"I remember. Traffic was chaos."

"And for dinner. It won't be dressy. This isn't Downton Abbey. Wear something casual elegant. Nice, but simple."

"Nice, but simple," echoed Maggie. What had she brought from Oxford that was "nice, but simple?"

"So we're all set?" Anne beamed at Maggie.

"Bear! What about Bear?"

"Bear? Oh. Ursula. Your cat. Mary Meadows can cat-sit for you. She was going to take care of Maud's Jack Russells, but Maud's daughter-in-law is here. Are you in this afternoon? I'll have her come by and you can brief her."

Maggie knew when she was defeated. Anne had everything covered.

"Tomorrow at 8:30, then," Anne grinned.

Susan Alexander

Chapter Two. Big Boy

Discovered by Alan Street at Frinton-on-Sea, Essex, G. elwesii 'Big Boy' rivals 'Long Drop' and 'Lanarth' for having the largest snowdrop flower. At the same time, the plant is not especially tall considering the size of its blooms, which have been measured to be as much as 2 in/5 cm. Fortunately, the snowdrop has strong scapes to support its out-sized flowers.

Big Boy' has well-shaped outer segments that narrow to a point at the apex and display fine green lines near the tips. The inner segments are a solid green.

Maggie was ready and enjoying a second mug of coffee, white, no sugar. What she would do without her morning caffeine, she did not know. Not that it was helping her with the book, but it was still an essential part of her daily ritual. Without it, she would probably be completely catatonic.

She was packed. Three pairs of pants, three sweaters, a nightgown, underwear and a plain black wool crepe dress for the dinner. Plus all the little pots and bottles it now seemed she needed to, if not defeat the aging process, at least try to hold it at bay.

Maggie's bright auburn hair which curled wildly if left on its own was caught back by a hair clip. She had ivory skin and deep green eyes and was often bemused that what were considered such liabilities when she was growing up—her skinniness and height and hair—were now deemed to be assets. At least if one were twenty.

Maggie heard tires crunch in the gravel in front of the cottage. It must be Anne in her Range Rover. Mary, the cat sitter, had been given instructions on the care and feeding of Bear and had the spare set of keys. She would be by later that morning. Maggie looked around for the cat, but she was off doing her Bear thing—probably sleeping—and would not understand Maggie's goodbye and promise to return by Sunday night anyhow.

The knocker sounded and Maggie opened the door to her friend, who looked bright and energetic in her quilted blue Barbour and coordinated wool slacks.

"Ready?" asked Anne.

"Ready," replied Maggie and realised her voice lacked enthusiasm.

"The condemned man ate a hearty breakfast."

Anne laughed. "Let's go then. We really are going to have a great time. You'll see."

Maggie shrugged on her jacket, an elegant olive green alpaca. She knew it was too fashionable for the country, but it was what she had, so tough tuna. She grabbed her small suitcase and rolled it out to the car.

"We're off!"

The Cotswolds were designated an AONB (Area of Outstanding Natural Beauty) that included bits of Oxfordshire, Gloucestershire, Worcestershire and some other shires Maggie could not remember. Despite its proximity to Oxford, she had never visited the region except to go to Anne's, as she usually preferred to go south to London when she left the university town. But the Cotswolds justly deserved their reputation for beauty, with rolling hills amongst which nestled picturesque villages built of the local golden limestone.

Maggie became aware that Anne was getting from village to village by hurtling along on one lane tracks, with an occasional narrow pullover to allow an oncoming car to pass. With the slopes and curves, she could not imagine navigating in rain or snow without four-wheel drive. But Anne was an expert driver and, in less than half an hour, they had reached the Rochford Inn.

As Anne had said, the Rochford Inn had originally been an 18th century coaching house, whose golden stone facade glowed, even in the weak February sunlight. The main inn building was gabled and had a restaurant, a comfortable lounge, a bar and the reception desk. The Markhams, the husband and wife who ran the hostelry, lived in apartments overhead.

Off to one side, the former stable block had been converted to a dozen guest rooms. Anne pulled into the car park and told Maggie, "I arranged for early check in. We can leave our bags, freshen up and then head to the Manor. It's just a quarter of a mile away."

Maggie's room was pleasantly traditional, with the doubtless obligatory hunting prints on the wall, a comfortable double bed, small desk and chair and a recently renovated bathroom with a stall shower.

"Lucky me," thought Maggie, who had yet to adapt to the free-standing British bathtub. When forced to sit in a bathtub and use a hand-held shower head on the end of a hose, tall Maggie inevitably created Noah-worthy floods.

A notice on the desk advertised free WiFi, but Anne had insisted Maggie leave her laptop behind.

"Really? You can't survive a couple of days without email and a browser? Pathetic!"

In a brief time, Maggie was ready and she and Anne took off. Barely a minute later, they were turning into a drive between two modest stone pillars. A simple wooden sign leaning against one of the gateposts announced, "The Snowdrop Garden at Rochford Manor."

The drive wove through some woods and Maggie began to see scattered clumps of small white flowers. They passed an old stone barn on a low rise which was surrounded by a blanket of white. A final couple of turns and they came out to a gravel parking area in front of an impressive Georgian country house built out of the ubiquitous local limestone.

"Here we are," Anne announced as she parked the Range Rover between a sleek, bottle-green Jaguar and a more pedestrian Ford Mondeo estate wagon.

The women got out and stood admiring the Manor. It was three stories tall when the gabled windows in the roof were included and had chimneys at each end. Anne was about to point out one of the Manor's architectural features to Maggie when a woman came around the corner of the house and strode over to greet them.

"Good morning," she said briskly. "I'm Lady Ainswick. You're here for the snowdrop weekend?"

Lady Ainswick was of medium height, thin, with wiry grey hair pulled back into a bun. Her face was devoid of makeup and smooth despite her sixty plus years. She wore a long, dark wool skirt and, Maggie supressed a smile, Wellies. A light blue twin set that matched her eyes could be glimpsed under her unbuttoned tweed jacket.

Anne introduced herself and explained that, in place of the unfortunate Mrs Wiggins, she had brought Professor Eliot, who was visiting from Oxford.

"Oh? A botanist?" asked Lady Ainswick hopefully.

"No, I'm afraid not," said Maggie apologetically. "Social scientist."

"Fortunately, we anticipated we'd have all sorts, from experts to novices."

"I'd definitely be considered a novice," admitted Maggie.

"We're gathering in the Study House," said Lady Ainswick and took off back in the direction she had come. Maggie and Anne followed.

They were led to a low building that lay on the far side of a formal garden, still bare except for some clumps of snowdrops that were scattered in various beds. At the end of the garden stood a large greenhouse. Beyond the greenhouse was a sizeable area surrounded by high stone walls, where Maggie heard a rooster crowing.

Maggie indicated the immaculately kept garden. "This must be spectacular in season."

"It's fairly spectacular now."

Anne pointed off to the left, where woods extended as far as Maggie could see. Beneath the trees, thousands of snowdrops were in bloom. They were everywhere, a dense carpet of white.

Wordsworth's "I wandered lonely as a cloud," came into Maggie's mind. "Those were daffodils, but they couldn't possibly have been more beautiful," she thought.

Then, "Good grief, Eliot. Poetry?"

Well, perhaps a little natural beauty was what she needed.

Lady Ainswick motioned them through a door. Inside was a large room, with a long refectory table in the centre and high-backed wooden chairs arranged on both sides. A laptop computer with a projector sat at one end and a projection screen had been erected at the other. Three walls of the room were a misty blue colour, with windows in the long wall letting in the sunlight. The wall opposite was covered with a mural of the Cotswold countryside in summer.

Against the muralled wall was a table holding a large urn of hot water. Blue Willow cups and saucers were laid out, along with a plate of tea bags, a pitcher of milk, a sugar bowl and a jar of instant coffee.

"Instant? Oh dear," thought Maggie. "Good thing I got my fix before I left."

She glanced at Anne and realised her friend had also seen the regrettable jar.

Standing in front of the table, holding cups of tea, were a comfortably dressed, pleasant-looking couple closer to seventy than sixty. At the far end of the table stood another woman, cupless, studying the mural. In her late forties, Maggie guessed, but with work done, she wore a red wool suit that showed off good skin and dark brown hair and eyes. Beneath the jacket she wore a white silk blouse and strands of serious pearls.

Lady Ainswick made the introductions. "Mrs Brooks, Professor Eliot, may I present Mr and Mrs Townsend, from Devon, and Mrs Ashbury, from Chipping Norton."

Mrs Townsend held out her hand. "Call me Daphne, please," she said in a gentle voice. "And this is Graham," she indicated her husband.

Anne took her hand. "I'm Anne," she said. "And this is Maggie."

Maggie also shook hands, but noticed Mrs Ashbury had kept her place and merely nodded aloofly.

"Chipping Norton?" Anne asked innocently. "Isn't that a hotbed of dodgy media moguls and even dodgier politicians? And where that TV person, Jeremy someone, lives?"

"Oh yes, Jeremy Clarkson. The car man. I thought it sounded familiar," said Daphne Townsend.

Mrs Ashbury gave a brittle smile and spoke in a throaty, smoker's voice. "Unfortunately, one cannot always choose one's neighbours…"

Her remark was interrupted by the entrance of three men. One was ancient, with a bald crown covered with liver spots and tufts of white hair sticking out from all sides, including his ears and nose. Hands that were equally spotted held a cane, but blue eyes behind wire-rimmed glasses were sharp and bright. He wore tweeds that looked as old as he did and similarly well-worn brogues.

"Lady Ainswick," he beamed.

"Professor Wolford;" Lady Ainswick smiled.

"Everyone, please, may I introduce Phineas Wolford, Cambridge Professor Emeritus and author of *Stalking the Wild Galanthus*. Phineas, how are you?"

"Never better, Lady Ainswick, never better."

The two other men stepped forward. Dark-haired, attractive and in their thirties, they were dressed almost identically in corduroy trousers, plaid flannel shirts, shooting jackets and Timberlands. Maggie concluded they must be Anne's Derek and Damian.

Anne made the introductions herself. "Lady Ainswick, this is Derek Fiske and Damien Hawking. They are exceptional garden designers who are based in Burford. The show garden they designed for the National Cancer Research Fund won a silver award at the Chelsea Flower Show last year."

The Townsends offered their congratulations and even Mrs Ashbury looked impressed.

Another couple stood in the doorway and peered into the room.

"And you must be the Puseys," said Lady Ainswick, moving forward to welcome the new arrivals.

The man nodded. "That's right. Sarah and George Pusey. Is this the snowdrop seminar?"

He had a strong regional accent Maggie could not identify.

"Midlands," Anne enlightened Maggie.

George Pusey wore an inexpensive grey suit that needed pressing, covered by an equally wrinkled navy blue trench coat. In his thirties, he was slightly shorter than Maggie and had a soft body and pasty complexion.

Sarah Pusey was a good ten years younger than her husband, had over-bleached blonde hair and hard features under too much make up. She had on black pants made of a shiny, synthetic material and a black seaman's jacket. She wore trainers and carried a large black handbag, its surface covered with rows of silver-coloured, circular metal studs.

"Not exactly whom you'd expect," murmured Anne.

Once more, introductions were made.

"At least this way I may remember people's names," Maggie decided.

A woman carrying a plate of biscuits came in quietly through a door behind the projection screen. She put the plate on the table and looked inquiringly at Lady Ainswick.

"Everyone, this is Charlotte. Charlotte Verney. If there is anything you need, please ask her."

Charlotte smiled briefly, then looked down at the floor. She was in her late twenties and could have been quite pretty if she had taken the trouble, but she looked washed out and tired. When no one made any requests, she retreated.

"Lady's Ainswick's family name is Verney. She must be a relative," Anne told Maggie.

While the group's attention had been fixed on Charlotte, another man had entered. He was about Maggie's height, somewhat stocky, with thinning, pale blond hair and light grey eyes. He was dressed similarly to Derek and Damien, but where their clothes were tailored and carefully kept, his corduroy pants bagged and his flannel shirt showed signs of frequent washing.

Lady Ainswick saw him and exclaimed, "Geoff! Everyone, this is Geoff Mortimer, who is responsible for overseeing our snowdrop programme here at Rochford Manor."

Again introductions were made. Lady Ainswick counted heads and glanced at her watch. "It's nearly ten, Geoff. I don't know where our two missing attendees are, but why don't you start? It's hardly fair to keep the ones who have been prompt waiting for those who are tardy."

"Has everyone had tea or coffee?" Geoff asked. "Then take a seat, please, and we'll begin."

Anne sat down next to Derek and Damien and Maggie sat next to Anne, with Graham and Daphne Townsend on her right. Professor Wolford, the Puseys and Mrs Ashbury took seats on the other side of the table. Maggie was amused when Mrs Ashbury waited to see if one of the men would pull out her chair for her. None did, so she yanked it out herself and sat down with a flounce and a frown.

Geoff Mortimer reviewed the plan for the weekend and then said, "Very well. Since we have people here ranging from beginners to experts, I will give a brief history of the Galanthus and then a more extended history of Rochford Manor.

"Professor Wolford, it is a privilege to have you with us today, so please feel free to expand on anything I may say. And you all have Rochford Manor folders with pads of paper and pens in front of you to take notes, if you desire."

Geoff turned on the projector and a title slide appeared. "A Brief History of the Snowdrop," it announced.

Geoff began, "No one knows with any certainty how the first snowdrops came to Britain. The earliest mention of a snowdrop in a written record was in the sixteenth century. Snowdrops were associated with the celebration of Candlemas on February second, which may explain why colonies of snowdrops are found in so many churchyards."

Maggie opened her folder and picked up the pen, then hesitated. Did she really want to take notes? No. She had been taking enough notes for her book. She put down the pen and settled in to listen. Maggie noticed she was not the only listener. While Daphne Townsend, Sarah Pusey, Violet Ashbury and Damien Hawking were note takers, the rest were sitting back and enjoying the presentation.

Geoff's was an interesting talk and he was an engaging speaker. He had just begun, "And now to tell you about Rochford Manor," when the outside door slammed open and the morning's light dimmed as a large figure filled the space.

A man strode into the room. He was massive, six feet, four inches at least, Maggie guessed, and, while not exactly fat, definitely had the beginnings of what she had heard referred to as "a corporation." He had an oversized, round head and was even balder than Professor Wolford, with his remaining hair shaved to a stubble. He had a ruddy complexion and a baby face which was emphasised by a little bow-lipped mouth, pursed into a pout.

Small eyes set too close together squinted and his jaw jutted forward. He reminded Maggie of a gigantic two-year old preparing to throw a tantrum. Like a book she'd read to one of her nephews when he was young. Megatot. That was it. *Megatot and the Robotty Potty Plot.*

"What, you couldn't have waited?" he demanded of the room at large. "You must have known I was attending."

An American by his accent, Maggie decided. Midatlantic, probably.

Lady Ainswick appeared from behind the screen. She looked the man over, then said, "You must be Ty Mitchell. I am sure you are sorry to be so late. Feel free to help yourself to some tea or coffee and then please take a seat."

Mitchell, still glowering, shook his head. He considered his options, then marched to take a chair at the top of the table, next to Violet Ashbury. It was his way of trying to maintain dominance of the room.

"What an asshole," whispered Maggie to Anne.

"I'll say," responded her friend.

"Geoff, please continue," said Lady Ainswick and drifted back to whatever was through the door behind the projection screen.

Geoff went on to tell the story of Rochford Manor and its gardens. The Ainswick interest in snowdrops began following the Crimean War, when the eighth viscount undertook several tours of the eastern Mediterranean and returned with a variety of specimens which he planted at the Manor. They multiplied and the collection grew.

"Thanks to the efforts of the Ainswicks, Rochford Manor currently has over two hundred different varieties of Galanthus."

Geoff was concluding his talk when the door once again opened and a woman entered. She took three steps, then paused.

"Strike the pose," thought Maggie.

The woman was tall, anorexically thin and wore a lush fur jacket that matched her champagne blonde hair.

"Mink?" wondered Maggie. "I hope no one here belongs to PETA."

The Ainswick Orange

Having assured herself that she had the attention of the room, she strutted forward in four-inch heels.

"God, have I had the trip from hell," she said in a rich contralto. "Do you call these things roads? The Rolls got stuck three times. I thought the driver would go postal."

Another American. An aging beauty with grey-green eyes, high cheekbones and a flawless complexion. Maggie thought her lips had had silicon injections, but whoever had done them had been good. Really good. Probably the same person who had done the Botox and Restylane. But for a woman on the wrong side of fifty, she didn't look a day over forty.

"Maggie, don't be such a bitch," she told herself.

Lady Ainswick once again appeared.

"Ah, finally. You must be…"

"Sylvia Biddle-Pew," the woman interrupted. "Hi there, Geoff. Your directions really sucked."

Lady Ainswick looked from one to the other. "You've met?"

"At the Royal Horticultural Society Show in London last week," explained Geoff.

"How nice," said Lady Ainswick mildly.

She checked her watch. "My. With the late start and interruptions, perhaps you should begin the tour, Geoff. You want to be on time for lunch at the inn."

Lady Ainswick glanced down at Sylvia Biddle-Pew's Louboutin's. She gave an almost imperceptible shake of her head, then left.

Geoff addressed the group. "Since the weather is so favourable, we want to take a preliminary tour of the gardens. An orientation, if you like."

He also noticed Sylvia's choice of shoes.

"Sylvia, parts of the garden are quite muddy and the paths through the trees can be slippery. Do you perhaps have alternative footwear?"

Sylvia formed her full lips into a pout. Then she sighed. "I may have packed my Prada sneakers. I'll check."

With twelve sets of eyes upon her, Sylvia Biddle-Pew turned and, with a runway model's swagger, left the room.

"Well," breathed Anne.

"Biddle. And Pew. Both old Philadelphia families. American aristocracy."

"And did you notice her lips?"

"Silicon?"

"Absolutely!"

Anne knew about these things. Maggie felt better about her uncharitable thoughts concerning Sylvia Biddle-Pew.

After what Maggie termed a potty break, the group reassembled outside. Geoff led them through the woods and pointed out the various varieties of snowdrops. Magnet. A fragrant field of S. Arnott. Hippolyta. Ophelia. Lord Lieutenant. Maggie decided she would never remember all the names nor how to tell one snowdrop from another and would just enjoy the spectacle.

Sylvia, having found her Pradas, clung to Geoff's arm. He gallantly helped her along the admittedly slippery paths, while Violet Ashbury attached herself to Ty Mitchell, to his mingled pleasure and unease.

"Call me Violet," she invited Ty.

"And people call me Mitch," he responded, standing taller and expanding his chest.

"Are we having fun yet?" Anne asked Maggie.

Susan Alexander

Chapter Three. Grumpy

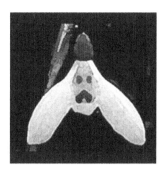

G. elwesii 'Grumpy' has plump flowers with a claw at the end of their broad outer segments. Inner markings that look like a scowling face, with two green eyes and a turned-down mouth, give the snowdrop its name. It is otherwise considered to be a fairly ordinary elwesii.

'Grumpy' was found in 1990 by Joe Sharman in the late Sir Vivian Fuchs' Cambridge gardens, where G. elwesii were naturalised. Sir Vivian is known for making the first surface crossing of Antarctica in 1957-1958

Lunch at the Rochford Inn was a pleasant affair. The group had divided themselves between two large tables. Maggie and Anne were joined by Derek and Damien, Ty—"call me Mitch"—and Violet, as well as Lady Ainswick herself.

"Lord Ainswick sends his apologies. He had an unfortunate episode with his heart recently and Dr Morgan says he still needs to rest. But he is looking forward to joining us for dinner tomorrow night."

Enjoying a perfectly cooked salmon filet in a mustardy sauce, Maggie learned that Mitch was a ("the") major American snowdrop dealer. He had a property in Connecticut where he bred and propagated his collection.

"I believe I can say I offer more varieties than any other source outside of the UK," he said pompously.

"Do you have a website?" Maggie asked. "I'm sure my mother would be interested."

"A website? No," Mitch frowned.

"Do you have a catalogue?"

"A catalogue? No." Mitch's frown deepened.

"So how do you take orders?" Maggie pressed.

"By mail. Or sometimes fax."

"And how do people know what you're selling and the prices?"

"I can mail or fax a list."

"Do you have a card?"

"A card?"

"You know. A business card? With your name? Address? Phone number? Fax?"

Mitch ran his hands over his jacket pockets. "No. But here."

Mitch withdrew a crumpled napkin from one pocket and a stub of a pencil from another. "Write down your mother's name and address and I'll send her a list."

Maggie tried hard not to roll her eyes and she could sense Anne stifling a laugh. Lady Ainswick was also looking bemused. Maggie waved the napkin and pencil away, took out one of her own cards and wrote on the back. She handed the card to Mitch.

"Here are her details. I'm sure she would be interested in putting in an order."

Mitch took the card begrudgingly and shoved it in a pocket.

"What a jerk!" Maggie thought. "However, I am not going to let him spoil my enjoyment of this excellent bread and butter pudding. With custard sauce, no less."

At the second table, Maggie overheard the group discussing the latest eBay auction of a rare snowdrop bulb for more than £700.

"If this keeps up, we will soon have bulbs going for £1,000," said Damien.

"Tulipmania," opined Graham Townsend.

"Tulipomania," responded Professor Wolford. "And your bulbs would have to fetch a lot more than £1,000 to reach Tulipomania levels. In 1637, a single bulb went for ten times the yearly income of a craftsman. Another bulb was traded for a house."

"But don't you think £700 is still a ridiculous amount to pay for, what, a small white flower?" argued George Pusey.

"Shh, George," said Sarah Pusey, her hand on George's arm. "I think everyone agrees £700 is too much."

"But why not?" challenged Sylvia Biddle-Pew. "A bulb could bring £5,000 or even £10,000 if it were rare enough. And if there were a demand. Supply. Demand. Why should snowdrops be different than any other market?"

"The forces of capitalism," agreed Graham.

"Rubbish," insisted George.

After lunch, the group straggled back to the lecture room. Maggie fought to keep awake through Geoff's talk,

"From Linnaeus to Lord Lieutenant: Naming Snowdrops," which seemed to consist mostly of Latin. Graham Townsend closed his eyes and his head drooped, while Professor Wolford snored softly. By three o'clock, Maggie would have paid as much for a proper cup of coffee as any rare Galanthus and she guessed from Anne's nodding head that her friend would as well.

Then Geoff announced. "It is time for our second garden visit. We are fortunate to have been invited to take a private tour of another notable Galanthus collection. Beaumatin's formal gardens are different than Rochford Manor's naturalised woodland settings. And Lord Raynham has produced several named Galanthus which are noteworthy."

"Another lord?" thought Maggie. "How very Jane Austen."

Geoff got the group up and herded them towards the door. He glanced at Sylvia.

"So we don't all need to take separate cars on our back lanes, we have organised a couple of vans to take us over. The ride will only take about twenty minutes."

In front of the Manor, two passenger vans were parked. Anne wrinkled her nose.

"If it were good enough for the Royal Wedding," Maggie teased.

Sylvia was not convinced.

"Ride in a van? Moi? I don't think so, Geoff. I'll take my car and follow you."

Violet Ashbury also felt a van would be beneath her. She turned to Sylvia with a pleading look.

"Would you have room for a passenger?" asked Violet hopefully.

At first it appeared that Sylvia would refuse, but then she looked at Violet's impressive ropes of pearls. She shrugged.

"Sure."

"Well," said Anne, as she and Maggie clambered into one of the vans.

"I fear we are just the hoi polloi," joked Maggie to Sarah Pusey, who was sitting behind her.

Sarah looked at her blankly. "Huh?"

"Hoi polloi? The huddled masses? Wretched and unwashed? Lumpenproletariat?"

"I don't get it," said Sarah.

"Shut up, Sheila, er, Sarah," said George briskly. To Maggie he said, "Good one. You got that right."

"Oh yeah. Right." The coin had finally dropped for Sarah.

"Rich bitches," she said contemptuously, as Violet and Sylvia sorted themselves in the back seat of the Rolls.

At that moment, a man emerged from Rochford Manor. White-blond haired, a bit pudgy and wearing a beautifully tailored dark blue suit, he walked over to where a silver grey Golf was parked.

Anne stared out the window at the man.

"I know him," she said to Maggie. "Now where... I know. He's a solicitor. He works with a friend of mine in

London. Specialises in trusts and estates. Named Percy. No, wait. It's not Percy, it's Peevey. Now why would he be here, I wonder?"

The vans took off, followed by Sylvia's stately Phantom.

Twenty minutes later, as Geoff had promised, the vans drove through a pair of impressive wrought iron gates and down a long, tree-lined drive to a remarkable country house. Maggie thought she could identify elements of Elizabethan, Jacobean, Georgian and Victorian Gothic in its various architectural features. The combination should have been outlandish but, somehow, it worked. Perhaps it was the unifying effect of the golden Cotswold stone.

As the vans pulled up and their passengers disembarked, a man came out of a door centred in the house's Georgian facade. He was tall and thin and wore country tweeds. Maggie guessed him to be about sixty, with handsome, chiselled features, short brown hair just beginning to go grey and piercing, bright blue eyes.

Anne nudged her. "Um, yum."

Maggie gave her a death glare, but Anne just giggled. Giggled!

The man spoke. "Welcome to Beaumatin. Lady Ainswick tells me you are galanthophiles here for a study weekend. She thought you would find it interesting to see some specimens used in a somewhat different setting than Rochford Manor, where the Galanthus are mostly naturalised. Here we use them in more formal gardens, which were laid out by the twenty-third Lord Raynham and his wife in the late nineteenth century.

"I am Raynham and I will be your host and guide. I am happy to answer any questions you may have. If you would please follow me."

Behind her, Maggie heard Violet whisper excitedly to Sylvia, "Raynham? That's Lord Raynham himself! He's something like the 27th baron. Just imagine. His wife died four years ago. Cancer. Sad, but he's now one of Britain's most eligible men."

"Really?" said Sylvia, clearly interested.

The women linked arms and set off after the baron.

"They remind me of the raptors in Jurassic Park," murmured Anne.

"Poor Lord Raynham," agreed Maggie.

"Oh, I'd assume being pursued by predatory women is not a new experience for him. I should think he can take care of himself."

Behind the grand house were a whole series of small gardens, divided by walls and hedges and steps leading to different levels. All were blooming with snowdrops, which were frequently partnered with other early flowering plants, like fuchsia pink cyclamen, burgundy red hellebores and bright yellow aconite. They contrasted appealingly with the small white flowers.

Maggie noticed the group had broken into clumps like the snowdrops themselves. Sylvia and Violet were still monopolising Lord Raynham, but had been joined by Geoff and Mitch. Anne was with Derek, Damien and the Townsends, while the Puseys appeared to be grilling Professor Wolford.

"What a strange, ill-assorted group," thought Maggie. "And I'm not sure any of them qualify as galanthophiles. Well, Professor Wolford. of course, and perhaps the Townsends. But the rest seem like they've only come because snowdrops are the current trend. Even Anne."

Maggie noticed a snowdrop labelled "Grumpy." She squatted down to look more closely. Carefully lifting one of the blossoms, she saw that indeed the green markings on the inner petals looked like a scowling face.

A pair of sturdy shoes and tweed-clad legs stopped beside her. Maggie looked up to see Lord Raynham. She tried to stand up quickly but teetered and he caught her elbow to steady her. The clasp that held her hair in place came loose and her curls exploded. Lord Raynham stared at her and Maggie flushed.

"Sorry." She extended a hand. "Maggie Eliot."

He took her hand and held it.

Maggie, flustered, hurried on. "Grumpy is good. I would recognise Grumpy again if I saw him. But Hippolyta and Ophelia and Titania? I'm not sure I could tell one from the other without their labels.

"A friend of mine makes Burgundy. Wine. In France. He says that the wines he sells the most to Brits and Americans are the ones whose names they can remember and pronounce. More Pommard than Aloxe Corton or Auxey Duresses. Is that true for snowdrops as well? Is Grumpy more popular than, um," she glanced down at a label, "Washfield Warham?"

"You'd need to ask Geoff Mortimer that. Rochford Manor sustains itself on plant sales. But let me show you one of our Galanthus you may find as memorable as little Grumpy there."

He took her elbow and led her to some small clumps under a birch tree. "Beaumatin's Harriet" read the label.

"It's yellow," Maggie stated the obvious. "Or at least parts are."

"Yes. Yellows are comparatively rare among Galanthus. There's Primrose Warburg, Wendy's Gold, Ecusson d'Or, Lady Elphinstone, Carolyn Elwes. But this is a double, which makes it even more exceptional."

"Beaumatin's Harriet. Is this yours? Did you develop, er, breed it here?"

He nodded. "There are rumours that there is an even rarer Galanthus at Rochford Manor. A true orange snowdrop. Have you seen it?"

Maggie shook her head. "No. And no one's mentioned it."

"It's probably too valuable to be in the public area. But keep your eye out. An orange would be something to see. Priceless."

He smiled down at her and his blue eyes were warm. "Another snowdrop you'd find hard to forget."

Violet came up and interrupted. "Lord Raynham? You need to come. Mr Mitchell thinks one of your Arnotts is showing signs of botrytis."

Lord Raynham looked like he'd heard bad news.

"Botrytis is a fungus. It kills snowdrops and gets into the soil. There's no treatment," he explained to Maggie.

"I should check." He left with Violet.

Maggie felt light-headed. She saw a bench and sat down. Anne joined her.

"Well! You had quite a little conversation. Tell me," she demanded.

Maggie shook her head. Her curls bobbled and she yanked them back and firmly refastened her hair clip.

What was she, fifteen years old? She had not had any sort of relationship with a man, except collegial ones, for six years. Since she had been given Bear, in fact. This was no time for her heart to go all fluttery. She was over all that. For good.

And for whom was she feeling so discombobulated? Some titled aristocrat? Good grief.

"Get a grip, Eliot! Just because he has the most extraordinary bright blue eyes..." she scolded herself.

"We discussed snowdrop varieties," she said as casually as she could. "He showed me one of the Beaumatin snowdrops. Harriet, it's called. Yellow. Very pretty."

She pointed it out to Anne, who gave her a "Yeah, right" look and glanced around.

"We'd better catch up with the others. We don't want to get left behind. Or maybe we do?" she teased.

The group was saying thank you's to Lord Raynham. He spoke to Maggie. "It wasn't botrytis. Mr Mitchell was mistaken."

"You must be relieved," said Maggie.

"Very," said Lord Raynham. He turned to Professor Wolford.

"So that's that," thought Maggie as she got in the van.

Susan Alexander

Chapter Four. Wendy's Gold

This yellow snowdrop was first discovered by Bill Clark at Wandlebury Ring in 1974 and noticed again by Esther Sharman ten years later. Its uniqueness was also recognised by her son, Joe, who alerted Clark.

Subsequently, twenty-seven bulbs were sold to the Dutch bulb company Geest for propagation. Twin-scaling increased the number to eight hundred, but then the entire lot was wiped out by botrytis. Fortunately, both Clark and Sharman had each kept single plants, while a third had been given to an associate. Current plants come from these three survivors.

One of the more robust yellows, with a strong stem, G. plicatus 'Wendy's Gold' has a yellow ovary and prominent yellow markings on its inner segments. The colour can vary from gold to chartreuse, depending on the amount of sun the plant receives. The snowdrop tends not to mature into clumps but distributes itself to give a spangled effect.

After a final lecture in the Study House that covered how to identify the main species of Galanthus, the group returned to the Rochford Inn to meet again for cocktails at seven o'clock. Maggie and Anne went to their rooms, where Maggie hoped to have a short nap.

However, she was too restless to sleep and her mind raced with all the new information she had tried to absorb throughout the day. And then there was Lord Raynham. No. She resolutely turned her thoughts away from the baron. Besides, she could not imagine she would ever see him again.

After twenty minutes, she gave up trying to sleep. There was nothing on television and she had no laptop. She washed her face, applied some lipstick, re-clipped her hair and went over to the main inn building.

Maggie found Violet Ashbury at the reception desk, talking in a low voice with Holly Markham. Holly ran the inn day-to-day, while her husband Mike acted as chef

Maggie heard Holly saying something about "Your card was declined," and Violet responding, "I'll pay in cash then. I assume cash is acceptable," before stalking off indignantly.

On the way out, Violet passed Sylvia Biddle-Pew, who was apparently checking in. Behind Sylvia came her driver. His arms were full of pillows and bed linens. Four Louis Vuitton suitcases were already piled on the floor in front of the reception desk.

Sylvia noticed Maggie's look of surprise and said, "I had planned to stay at someplace decent in the area, maybe the Barnsley House, but the trip this morning was just too ghastly. We got stuck three times and the Rolls got scratched.

"You'd think the Ainswicks, knowing who I am, would offer a room, but nooo. Apparently Lord Ainswick had a minor heart attack and is still recuperating. So here I am. In London, I'd be at the Dorchester. But here, in the country? Well, I suppose one must make sacrifices."

Maggie glanced at Holly. Behind Sylvia's back, Holly made a face and Maggie smiled.

"The Rochford Inn is perfectly nice, Sylvia. I'm sure you'll be fine. And think how much more convenient it will be."

THE AINSWICK ORANGE

Sylvia sniffed, then gestured at Holly. "Show Edwards the room. God, do I need a drink."

She grabbed the passing waitress. "Vodka rocks with a twist. I trust you have Grey Goose?"

The young woman nodded. She looked at Maggie. "Would you like something, ma'am?"

"A glass of the Sauvignon blanc, please." Maggie had already checked out the wine list.

"Large or small," asked the girl.

"Large," said Maggie decisively. She really, really wanted a drink. Her head felt like it was going to explode, not just with snowdrop trivia but with all the new people she had been meeting as well.

"Make that two, please," she heard Anne say from behind her.

"I'll bring them to you in the lounge," the waitress said and scurried off.

The women moved into a cosy room where a fire was burning. Comfortable leather armchairs were grouped around low tables. Professor Wolford was seated in one, a glass of sherry on the table before him. Mitch was standing in front of the fire, gesticulating with one hand and holding a glass of whisky with the other. From his flushed face, it looked like it was not his first.

"And I say we must do something about naming. Anyone who finds a Galanthus they hope is just a little different immediately names it after their Aunt Ermitrude or their old dog Wilfred and registers it. We'll soon have one thousand varieties or even more and who'll know which is which? Or how to value them?"

Anne said, "Well, day lilies, hemerocallis, have around forty thousand, or it could even be sixty thousand, I forget, named varieties. But only the best ones are available commercially. Let the market decide. Isn't that what you said at lunch, Sylvia?"

Sylvia nodded. "It's Darwinian. Survival of the fittest."

Maggie looked at Sylvia. All the Restylane in the world could not eliminate the hardness of her eyes.

The waitress arrived with their drinks and Maggie took a big sip, then sat and took a smaller one. In her current mood she would need to be careful or she would be tipsy before they had dinner.

Maggie noticed Sarah Pusey, sitting alone in a far corner and speaking quietly into her phone. She had changed into a red top with the sequined message, "Eat Your Heart Out," and skin-tight jeans, no, jeggings Maggie had heard them called.

What was with this woman? Maggie wondered. She could not believe she had any interest in snowdrops. And why had George called her Sheila? Was it a pet name? But then he had quickly corrected himself. There was something funny here. Maybe they were spies from a rival snowdrop grower. Except you would think a competitor would have sent people who would fit in more. Like the Townsends.

Maggie's attention was caught by Violet Ashbury, standing poised in the doorway and waiting to be noticed. She had changed into a light grey satin blouse and a deep purple wool skirt. The pearls still hung in strands down to her breasts. She was not a beauty like Sylvia Biddle Pew, but she was attractive enough. Lady Ainswick had called her Mrs, but Maggie did not see a wedding ring. Divorced, perhaps?

The Ainswick Orange

Miffed that the group's attention was still being monopolised by Mitch, Violet tossed her head and came into the room. She sat down on the arm of Anne's chair and looked around for the waitress, who had left to fetch Mitch another Glenlivet. She frowned.

In strolled George Pusey, carrying a pint of the local ale. He had changed into a more casual outfit of navy trousers and a brightly patterned sweater that became him better than his suit. He nodded to the group but went over to join Sarah, who had finished her call.

Last to join were Derek, Damien and the Townsends, who entered in the middle of Mitch's on-going monologue that had moved on from which plants worked best with snowdrops to the biases of the judges at last year's Chelsea Flower Show. The circle was widened and chairs were dragged over to accommodate the newcomers. The Puseys also took the opportunity to join the group.

"Hail, hail, the gang's all here," said Sylvia, who was finishing her second vodka rocks, Maggie noticed. The waitress came for additional drink orders and she requested a third. Maggie decided she had better nurse her second glass of wine and Anne did the same.

"Well," said Daphne Townsend, looking around. "Isn't this nice. I don't know about the rest of you, but I really enjoyed the lectures. And the garden visits, they gave Graham and me some wonderful ideas that we want to try at home."

Mitch snorted and was about to sound off again, but Anne intervened. "Where is home, Daphne?"

"Devon, near Newton Abbot. We moved from London when Graham retired from the City, so we could be nearer to our youngest daughter and her family."

Graham added, "I do miss London. Devon's pretty quiet in comparison. But Daphne finally has the garden she's always wanted, so I guess that's some compensation. And of course it's nice being able to see Abby and the grandchildren more often."

At the stroke of seven, Lady Ainswick entered, followed by Geoff Mortimer, Lord Raynham and a young woman who was a stranger to Maggie.

"Good evening all," said Lady Ainswick. "I must apologise for Lord Ainswick's absence, but both Dr Morgan and I felt that an additional day of rest was advisable. Lord Raynham has kindly agreed to serve as his stand-in. And I would like to present my daughter, Chloe Symeon."

Chloe Symeon was in her late twenties and probably looked much like her mother at that age, pretty and slender, with brown hair and blue eyes. Unlike her mother, who was still dressed in the country outfit she had worn earlier, Chloe was wearing an obviously expensive suit and flashed a large diamond engagement ring on the appropriate finger.

Having convinced herself that she would never meet the man again, Maggie was surprised to see Lord Raynham. He caught her startled expression, nodded slightly, and turned to give his order to the waitress. Maggie flushed in embarrassment, which made her feel even more self-conscious. Sensing Anne watching her, she gave her friend a look which said, "Don't!"

Lady Ainswick and Lord Raynham asked for whisky, while Chloe joined Violet with a gin and tonic. With Lady Ainswick present, the group's conversation had become more subdued and general, with remarks about the unusually mild weather featuring prominently.

"Everyone's on their best behaviour," Maggie murmured to her friend.

"And his Mitchness has finally shut up," noted Anne.

In fact, Mitch had fallen quiet and was staring morosely into the fire. However, it was not for long.

"Tell me, Lady Ainswick. I heard reports in London that you actually have a true orange snowdrop at Rochford Manor. It's said it's called the Ainswick Orange."

Geoff stiffened and Lady Ainswick went very still. The room became so quiet you could hear the proverbial pin drop. Maggie remembered Lord Raynham had also mentioned the rumour of an orange snowdrop.

Then Lady Ainswick said. "I am afraid we do not comment on any Galanthus which has not been publicly presented."

Mitch insisted, "So that's a yes?"

He looked eager, almost greedy.

"No," said Geoff firmly. "That's a no comment."

Maggie thought Geoff seemed nervous. She noticed Lady Ainswick looking at him pensively. Then the viscountess stood and announced, "I believe we are all ready for some dinner. I took the liberty of making place cards. You should find yours easily, but if you can't, please just ask."

She rose and led the group into the next room, where two round tables were set, each with eight places. Lady Ainswick took a place at one and said, "Phineas, you're sitting next to me." She indicated the seat to her right.

"Mr Mitchell, you are here, if you please," she gestured to her left.

Maggie read her card. "Professor Eliot." She was disconcerted to realise she was sitting to the right of "The Lord Raynham," as his place card was addressed, and was glad that Anne, as "Mrs Brooks," was on his left. George Pusey was on her right. Violet looked less than thrilled to be sitting between Graham Townsend and Damien Hawking. Chloe Symeon was more discrete about how she felt about being between Graham Townsend and George Pusey.

"Boy, girl, boy, girl" thought Maggie. "How very proper. Will we make conversation to the person on our left for ten minutes and then turn to the person on our right?"

Lord Raynham pulled out her chair for her and said, "Well, Professor Margaret Spence Eliot. Appleton Fellow at Merrion College. Formerly of Harvard University. Expert in cultural integration. You have some controversial views, apparently."

Maggie looked up at him in surprise. He sat down and said, "Lady Ainswick gave me a list of the people who would be here tonight. I googled you. You even have a page in Wikipedia. And some books on Amazon. And tens of thousands of other hits."

Maggie shook her head in embarrassment. "It's the citations. Academics have to publish and then other people reference you in their work. Speak at a few conferences and, voila, you're all over the Internet. Have you ever googled yourself?"

"No. I prefer to remain in blissful ignorance."

"It's funny. My grandmother used to tell me that a lady should be mentioned in the press only three times during her life. At her birth, her marriage and her death. I wonder what she'd think about today's passion for celebrity?"

"The same as my grandmother. She'd be horrified."

Maggie laughed. "No doubt."

She paused and groped for something more to say. "Thank you for the tour of your gardens today. They are quite wonderful."

Then she grimaced. "Sorry. I didn't mean to be so trite. I'm sure people tell you how wonderful they are all the time."

"In fact, at times they can feel like a heavy responsibility. It takes a lot of work to keep them up. I have help, but the estate is quite a full-time occupation. So it is nice to hear that others appreciate them. Are you a gardener?"

"Not unless you count a few pots of herbs in the kitchen and an orchid on a windowsill. I have always lived in a flat."

"Then, if you don't mind my asking, why are you here?"

"I'm supporting my friend Anne." She explained about the sabbatical, the writer's block, the vacant cottage and the gall stones.

Lord Raynham laughed. "Well, apologies to the sufferer, but I never thought I'd be thankful someone had gall stones."

While Maggie tried frantically to think of an appropriate response, Lord Raynham turned to Anne and she was left to talk to George Pusey.

"Exactly like Jane Austen," she decided.

Pusey was disinclined to converse. He preferred to concentrate on his food and gave the impression that he would have enjoyed his ale much more than the wines that accompanied the meal.

On the other side of the table, Chloe was listening politely to Graham Townsend talk about Devon, while Violet and Damien were comparing notes on an art exhibit both had recently seen in London.

At the second table, Maggie overheard Mitch ranting against the fashion for ornamental grasses, which was hotly defended by Derek.

Mitch countered with, "And you won a silver at Chelsea. You know, you boys were up for a silver-gilt or possibly a gold except, well, someone who must not be named suggested to a couple of the judges that you had dropped your drawers and grabbed your ankles to get votes. Too bad, but as long as you've got so many of those flaming old queens on the panel, it's a natural assumption."

A shocked silence followed. Then Anne turned to Lord Raynham and said in an acid voice that carried, "Well, it's always nice to know when a stereotype is true. About Americans, I mean. Of course, I believe assholes are a worldwide occurrence. Or so my husband tells me. He's an expert in global development, so he'd know."

While it seemed impossible, given its already flushed state, Mitch's complexion turned such a deep beet red that Maggie was afraid he was going to have a stroke.

"Not that that would be such a bad thing," she thought. "At least it would shut him up."

Mitch threw his napkin down on the table, excused himself and staggered towards the restrooms. The room seemed to give a collective sigh of relief.

Lord Raynham had turned back to her and Maggie commented, "I always thought gardening was supposed to promote serenity, but this seems more like a college faculty meeting."

"You mean the gossip and the petty rivalries and the viciousness?"

Maggie nodded.

"Yes, things can get pretty heated. And then there are the collectors."

"The collectors?"

"People who have to have the rarest, the most recently discovered specimens. They can be completely unscrupulous. I've had a few of my most valuable plants stolen. So have the Ainswicks. One of the ones I lost was unique. A new discovery. A single plant. Someone came in and dug it up and walked off with it. After that I only put the more common plants out for public view. The rare ones are planted someplace not accessible to visitors and aren't labelled. I believe they do the same at Rochford Manor."

"I guess it's to be expected, with bulbs selling on eBay for hundreds of pounds."

"At least the eBay sales are honest."

"Rottweilers. You need Rottweilers," Maggie said. "And the equivalent of metal detectors for botanical material that your visitors must pass through before they leave. Or trained dogs, like the beagles at airport customs that sniff your bags for agricultural produce."

Lord Raynham laughed. Then grew serious. "If a few more bulbs change hands at these prices and the publicity keeps up in the media, we may have to do that."

Pusey broke in. "It's a disgrace. Throwing that kind of dosh at a flower, fer chrissake. People've got more money than sense."

"You're not a galanthophile, then?" Maggie asked.

"I like flowers, same as the next fellow. But…"

Maggie never found what Pusey would have said as, at that instant, a man entered the room. About forty, he had a face that would have been handsome except it was flushed and puffy from too much alcohol. He wore a double-breasted, dark blue blazer with gold crested buttons, tan trousers and a pink shirt that was slightly frayed at the cuffs.

Lady Ainswick had her back to the door and did not see the newcomer, but Chloe did. All the colour left her face and she gasped, "Edward! What the hell are you doing here?"

Lady Ainswick excused herself to Professor Wolford and slowly turned in her chair.

"Edward?" she said in a tone of incredulity.

"Yes," Edward smirked. "It is I. Hello, Mother. Hello, Chloe, my beloved sister. They told me at the house I could find you here. Oh. And I see you're here too, Raynham."

Maggie turned to Lord Raynham.

"Ainswick's son. Heir. Ne'er do well. He's supposed to be in Cyprus. I can't imagine why he's turned up here."

THE AINSWICK ORANGE

Edward Symeon addressed the party at large. "Sorry to interrupt. Please continue with your…" he peered down at a dish. "I guess it's pudding."

"Edward, answer the question. What are you doing here?"

"Well, Mother, I heard via the social media grapevine—the Internet is such a wonderful invention—that poor Father was not well at all and I felt it my duty, doo-tee, to come and find out how he was. I am, after all, the heir."

"As you can see," Lady Ainswick almost hissed, "I am in the middle of dinner. Why don't you wait in the lounge and I will join you there shortly. Have you seen your father?"

"Sadly, Mother, no. I tried, but dear Cousin Charlotte wouldn't open the door."

Lady Ainswick had no reply. She pressed her lips tightly together.

Edward reached in a jacket pocket, extracted a mobile phone and held it out to his mother.

"Why don't you call the house and tell them I am coming and that they should prepare a bed for me."

Lady Ainswick looked like she wanted to throw the phone at his head. Instead she said coldly, "I have my own phone, thank you."

She excused herself and left the room. A minute later she returned.

"You are fortunate. The inn has a room available. You can stay here and not cause any inconvenience at the house. Or disturb your father at this hour."

She handed him a key.

"Oh, I'm sorry. I wouldn't want to be an inconvenience. Well, see you tomorrow, then, Mother. And my dearest sister. And you, Raynham." There was loathing in his voice when he said the baron's name.

Edward turned to the company and gave a mock bow. "Good night, all."

Lady Ainswick remained standing, her expression stern, until Edward left. When he had gone, Lady Ainswick sat back down and said to Professor Wolford, "I'm sorry for the interruption, Phineas. You were saying?"

Some colour had returned to Chloe's face. She said to the table. "Apologies for the sib. I hope it's the only one I'll have to make for him. He really shouldn't be here."

Anne, feeling that etiquette had been sufficiently shattered, leaned forward and said to Maggie, "It's common knowledge, so I don't expect I'm repeating gossip," she glanced at Chloe, who was talking to Damien. "But Edward, well, after some years of his creating scandals and making unsustainable inroads on the family fortune, the family set up a trust that pays him on the condition he live outside the UK. I believe he's settled in Cyprus."

Lord Raynham added, "It is a time-honoured tradition of how families deal with black sheep. They get their monthly remittance as long as they stay away."

"But he hasn't stayed away. He's come back." Maggie stated the obvious.

"Indeed."

Lady Ainswick rose. "I believe Mrs Markham has proposed coffee and after dinner drinks in the lounge. If you will excuse me, I must get back to the Manor. Chloe, you should stay if you wish."

"No. I'll come with you, Mother."

"Very well. I look forward to seeing you all again in the morning."

Mother and daughter left. Mitch had still not returned. Lord Raynham turned to Anne and Maggie.

"I also need to wish you good evening. But I'll be attending tomorrow. Dr Wolford is always good value once he gets going and Geoff is going to talk about yellow snowdrops, which are one of our specialities at Beaumatin."

After he departed, Anne eyed Maggie. "Well, well, well. Do you really think Geoff has anything to teach him about yellow snowdrops? Or could it possibly be something else that interests him at the seminar?"

Maggie looked at her friend blankly, then got her meaning.

"I really doubt it," she said firmly.

"Well, we shall see. But I haven't been attending faculty parties for three decades not to recognise the symptoms of incipient smitteness when I see them," said Anne confidently.

Susan Alexander

Chapter Five. Sentinel

Robust and elegant, 'Sentinel' frequently has two scapes with enlarged tips from which hang its large blooms. The outer segments have heavily-ridged surfaces, while the inner segments have top and bottom markings of green, separated by a white band. Stems that stand upright at attention give this snowdrop its name.

'Sentinel' was discovered by Daphne Chappell in the former Backhouse gardens at Sutton Court, Herefordshire, in 1994.

Maggie was too wound up to go to bed. She told herself that it was because, after weeks alone in the cottage, she was over-stimulated from the day's events. It certainly had nothing at all to do with a particular pair of bright blue eyes.

"Only a lesser woman would become infatuated with someone merely on the basis of some polite words and a smile, and I am not a lesser woman," she reminded herself.

She decided she would go outside for a while. Perhaps some fresh air would make her feel sleepy. She had noticed a bench besides some children's play equipment at the edge of the old stable block where the guest rooms were. She could sit there and enjoy the unseasonably mild night.

The lights were out in the front of the main inn building, although Maggie assumed there was still clean up going on in the kitchen in the rear. While some of the guest rooms were dark, others showed lights and several windows were open. Voices carried.

Maggie heard Violet Ashbury. All the huskiness had left her voice. Instead it sounded harsh and strident.

"Philip, you bastard! Your alimony cheque bounced. My bank card's been frozen."

There was a pause while Philip presumably reacted.

"I don't care if the markets have been difficult. I've been seriously embarrassed."

Another pause.

"Why should I sell the house? I'm not the one who got the hots for his dental hygienist, the little bitch."

Maggie could almost hear Violet pacing.

"Pay up, Philip, or the next call you get will be from the court!"

"Oh my," thought Maggie. So her guess that Violet was divorced had been correct. And that's what the conversation she had overheard about Violet's card being declined had concerned. Poor Violet. Maggie was more thankful than ever that she was single and financially self-sufficient.

Other voices carried in the night air.

"Derek! I just talked to Sean. And he confirmed it. Guess who screwed us out of a gold at Chelsea?"

"Who?"

"That walking butthole."

"Mitch the bitch?"

"Uh huh."

"That prick! I'm going to kill him! Kill him!"

"No, you can't. I have firsties."

"Slowly and painfully. Something medieval. Like molten lead up his arse. Same as they did to that king in that play. King Whatshisname."

"You really should have studied harder at school, Derek."

"I'll fix him, I will. Do you know what a gold would have done for us?"

"Derek, don't cry. Come on. Remember, what goes around comes around."

"Oh dear," Maggie thought. Mitch really was a horrible person. But Damien was right. What goes around would come around. It was simply a matter of time.

She heard a second woman's voice.

"I certainly think it has been worth coming. Don't you, Graham?"

It was Daphne Townsend. Her husband's response was indistinct.

"And your fears that someone would remember you. I really believe that's finally behind us now. And you were never the actual wrongdoer anyway. I think you should stop worrying so much."

Again, Maggie could not make out Graham's reply. Still, she was intrigued. Did Graham Townsend have a guilty secret? A sordid past? She remembered thinking earlier that the Townsends would make excellent snowdrop spies. But Daphne was referring to something that had happened previously. Maggie was sorry she had yielded to Anne's demand that she leave her laptop at the cottage. Her fingers itched to google Graham Townsend.

Maggie heard Daphne ask, "Do you have a copy of our snowdrop order, Graham? I want to make sure we ordered several of the…" when her gentle voice was obscured by another woman's.

"So tomorrow is the big day, George. I think it will be tomorrow. There should really be some action. Old Lady Ainswick's gonna tear out her hair."

It was Sarah Pusey.

"…. do something?"

It was a man's voice. Maggie assumed it must be George Pusey.

"Do what? It's not like I have proof."

"Then warn someone?"

"And spoil all the fun? No way."

Before Maggie could spend much time speculating about what might be happening the next day, she was distracted by someone moving stealthily past the main inn building. An overhead light shone on blond hair. It was Geoff Mortimer.

"What's he doing here? Did he forget something at dinner? And why is he being so sneaky?" Maggie wondered.

But Geoff did not stop at the inn's front door. He continued on to the stable block with its guest rooms. He paused in front of a door and knocked softly. The door opened and Maggie saw the champagne mane of Sylvia Biddle-Pew.

"Hello, big boy." Sylvia plastered her body up against the botanist's and gave him a smouldering kiss.

Geoff entered quickly and the door closed. It remained closed until Maggie finally felt sleepy enough to return to her room. She certainly had enough to think about and to take her mind off the baron. And if she dreamed of bright blue eyes, well, she couldn't control what she dreamed, could she?

Susan Alexander

Chapter Six. The Ainswick Orange

G. 'Ainswick Orange' was discovered by Lord Ainswick on a trip to Sellafield in 2010. A true orange snowdrop, it has an orange ovary and orange markings on its inner segments. Paddle-shaped, widely spaced outer segments make the inner markings clearly visible. Only the single plant is known to exist.

The next day dawned cloudless and mild.

"Just another perfect day in paradise," Maggie thought to herself.

She showered and dressed and, desperate for caffeine, made her way to the inn's dining room. She found Anne there before her, a pot of coffee already on the table. Maggie was glad to discover they were the first ones there.

"After all that happened yesterday, I can't imagine what today will be like," said Maggie.

"I hope that dreadful Mitch is too hung over to turn up. Or maybe he packed his bags in the night and skulked off. What an awful human being."

Maggie had to agree: As Anne made her way through a "full English," as she liked to call her meal of eggs, bacon, sausage, beans, mushrooms, tomato and toast, and Maggie enjoyed scrambled eggs with smoked salmon, it seemed Mitch might well have left. Or at least it appeared that he was skipping breakfast.

The women had final cups of coffee. They returned to their rooms, washed and met in the car park, where they found they had more than an hour before the first lecture.

"Remember Lady Ainswick said we were welcome to wander around the grounds? Why don't we? It's a beautiful morning and we'll be sitting inside today a lot as it is," proposed Anne.

"That's fine with me," Maggie agreed.

They drove over to the estate, where theirs was the first car in the parking area in front of the house.

Maggie and Anne began with a walk through the snowdrop woods. Maggie tried to see if she could distinguish between snowdrop varieties, while Anne wondered if she could ever get such a carpet to grow under the trees at her home. After a while they exhausted the area they had visited the day before, but still had some time to spare.

"You know," said Maggie thoughtfully. "I wonder about something Lord Raynham said, about having the rarer varieties in a separate area. Want to see if we can find it? Do you think anyone would mind?"

"I don't see why. It's not like we'd steal a snowdrop or tell any of the others."

"Lead on then," said Maggie.

"That's my girl," said Anne. "Always up for an adventure."

They walked past the greenhouse to the walled garden. They peeked in but saw only chickens and some vegetable plots, freshly dug up and waiting for their spring planting.

"Maybe a bit further," said Anne.

The Ainswick Orange

Beyond the walled garden, the woods began again. There was a brief rise and then the ground sloped down gently to a dale scattered with trees. Paths had been laid out between cultivated beds where snowdrops were growing. The area was not visible from the places where the tour groups went and was well out of sight of the residence and the Study House. But there was no fence or other obstacle to keep out the curious.

"I think we found it!" Anne was excited.

Maggie looked at a clump of snowdrops. It was unlabelled. The flowers were long-petalled and streaked with green.

She turned to Anne.

"I guess they protect them by eliminating the markers," she said.

The friends walked down a path and turned a corner.

A body lay sprawled out, crushing the snowdrops beneath it. One outstretched hand gripped a gardening trowel and just out of reach was a freshly dug hole nearly a foot deep. The back of the man's head had been smashed in and grey brain matter oozed from between shattered pieces of skull. A face was turned towards them, grey-tinged beneath its usual flush.

It was Mitch.

He looked surprised and somehow foolish. His lips were slightly pursed and, with his protruding eyes, he reminded Maggie of a stuffed fish her father had had hanging on his study wall.

Then Maggie saw little black specks before her eyes like a swarm of gnats.

Anne made a sound like "Eurk" and ran a little ways off. Maggie heard her vomiting, but could not take her eyes off the corpse. She noticed that a hefty rock flecked with blood and skin and some bits of stuff she preferred not to think about lay a few feet away.

"Anne?" she said, finally able to back away from the dead man.

Anne had taken a bottle of water from her large handbag and was rinsing her mouth. Anne was always prepared.

"We need to tell the Ainswicks. And then call the police."

"Shouldn't we just call the police?" asked Maggie, thinking of the crime shows she liked to watch on television.

Anne gave her a look like she was being very dim and checked her mobile.

"Damn. No reception. How about you?"

Maggie looked. "No."

"If I go back to the house, do you mind waiting here? I don't think anyone is lurking around. But someone should…"

"Stay with the body. I know. And not touch anything."

Anne smiled grimly. "Yes."

While neither woman would admit it, if they'd had to come across one of their group murdered, Mitch would certainly have been their choice.

"But no one deserves this," thought Maggie.

The Ainswick Orange

"I'll be back just as soon as I can. If there's a problem, well, scream your head off and run like crazy."

"I can do that," Maggie promised.

Anne hurried back the way they'd come. Maggie thought she would be all right if she stayed a bit further away from the corpse. She backed off and was careful where she stepped, but did not see any footprints or anything else that might be evidence—a cigarette butt or gum wrapper or orange peel or piece of cloth.

A minute passed. A movement between some distant trees caught her eye. She looked and saw someone move from one trunk to another.

Maggie thought her heart would burst, it was beating so fast.

"Hello?" she called out, while looking around for any possible way to defend herself.

"Hello? Who's there?"

A young girl stepped out from behind a large elm. Maggie guessed her age to be around ten. It was Saturday, so there would have been no school.

The girl had long brown hair pulled back in a braid and big brown eyes. She was wearing jeans and trainers and a blue, down-filled jacket. She looked very serious and reminded Maggie of someone.

The girl walked over to Maggie. She stared at Mitch's body.

"He's dead?"

Maggie nodded. The child really should not be here, but Maggie knew she could not leave to take her elsewhere. Surely Anne would be back soon.

"I'm Maggie. Maggie Eliot. Who are you?"

"Emily Verney."

Maggie thought hard. Verney.

"Is Charlotte your mother?"

Emily nodded.

"Do you know where she is?"

"Getting things ready."

"Do you think you could go tell her, tell her what's happened and to check that the police have been called?"

The girl stared at Maggie without expression, then turned and walked off towards the house.

After what seemed like hours but was doubtless minutes, Maggie heard voices. Anne was approaching, with Lady Ainswick, Lord Raynham and Geoff Mortimer.

Geoff reached Maggie first.

"Where?" he asked, then saw for himself.

"Oh God."

Lady Ainswick joined them. She looked at the body, then moved closer.

"Geoff?" she said, her voice sounding quavery and old. "Geoff? Where is the Ainswick Orange?"

She collapsed and Geoff and Anne rushed forward to catch her.

Maggie also started towards Lady Ainswick, but Lord Raynham caught her arm.

"Two are enough, I think," he explained. "What happened?"

"I don't know. Anne, Mrs Brooks, and I arrived early and decided to walk around the grounds. We ended up here and found…" she gestured.

"Mitch. Er, Mr Mitchell. Like that. He was obviously dead, so we didn't touch anything. Have the police been called?"

"Yes. Miss Symeon is waiting for them and will bring them here."

Lady Ainswick had revived and looked bewildered. Then she glanced down and saw Mitch. Her face crumpled.

Anne offered to take her back to the house.

"Better stay here. I'm sure the police will want to talk to whoever found the body," Anne said to Maggie as she passed, supporting Lady Ainswick with Geoff's help.

Maggie nodded. She closed her eyes and felt Lord Raynham's hand at her elbow.

"Are you all right? You must be in a state of shock."

"It was a shock, but… I guess they're right. About all those TV shows making one immune to violence. It didn't seem real…"

Maggie glanced over at the body. "It still doesn't seem real. And the way he fell. Holding that trowel. Do you think he had come to steal the snowdrop?"

"From the looks of that hole, I'd say a snowdrop may have been taken. And we both heard Lady Ainswick mention the Ainswick Orange before she fainted."

"An orange snowdrop. You mentioned that. And Mitch asked about it before dinner last night. Do you think Mitch surprised the thief?"

"Or one thief surprised another thief. Mr Mitchell didn't have that trowel by accident."

Maggie considered this. "Who would do something like this?"

Lord Raynham shrugged. "The grounds are open. Anyone could have come in."

"Do you really think it was a stranger, an outsider? Who took that particular snowdrop, when there are so many others that are easier to take? Even here, in this remote area?"

"I would rather think it was not someone from your group or anyone else I knew. And it would certainly be preferable," Lord Raynham said finally.

"Preferable to all of us being considered as suspects, do you mean?"

"Very good, Professor Eliot. Yes. Being suspected by the police is not a pleasant experience."

"That sounds as if you know what that's like."

"My older brother. Charles. We were both at home at Beaumatin. He'd been drinking. Heavily. He fell down the stairs. Broke his neck. He was twenty-four. The police inspector who was investigating became convinced there was, er, foul play and the coroner's inquest came back with a verdict of Open Death.

"Since Charles' death meant I would come into the title, I was on the top of the inspector's list of suspects. His only suspect, in fact. In the end there was no proof it wasn't an accident. But an investigation... You have no idea."

"I'm so sorry," Maggie impulsively put her hand on Lord Raynham's arm. "It must have been dreadful."

Lord Raynham was silent. But he put his hand over Maggie's.

"What is taking the police so long?" she asked somewhat plaintively.

"They have to come from Cheltenham at least. Possibly as far as Gloucester. Even if they left as soon as they got the call, it will take them twenty, twenty-five minutes. Or longer."

They stood quietly. Maggie was thinking. Finally, she said, "Well, presumably, whoever killed Mitch also took the Ainswick Orange. So the thing to do would be to find the snowdrop."

Thomas looked at her quizzically. "And how would you do that?"

"I guess I would start by searching people's stuff."

"And supposing the person planted it someplace out of the way, with the intention of retrieving it later."

"But wouldn't an orange snowdrop be fairly obvious?"

"What do you think an orange snowdrop looks like? A small plant with bright orange flowers? Yes, that might stand out at this time of year. But, in fact, it wouldn't look like that at all. Here, come look at this."

He led her twenty feet further away from the body.

"Do you see this Galanthus? It's a very rare yellow, named Carolyn Elwes. See the yellow ovary and the yellow on the inner segments? It's called a yellow snowdrop, but, from a distance all you would see is a small white flower. Only if you were up close would you notice the yellow."

"So you think the Ainswick Orange would have an orange—you called it an ovary? And maybe some orange on the petals?"

"That would be my assumption. And it may or may not have markings on the segments. Or only on the inside where they would not be so obvious. See, here are some Primrose Warburgs, next to the Carolyn Elwes. They were probably put here to confuse poachers. Only an expert could tell which was which."

"So what you're saying is that the thief might have hidden the plant in plain sight?"

"That's what I'd do. And it would make it harder to prove who had actually taken it. No smoking gun, I believe you Americans would say."

At that moment, Maggie heard voices. A group of men were approaching, accompanied by Lady Ainswick and Geoff Mortimer.

"Ah. The Gloucestershire Constabulary have arrived," said Lord Raynham.

The Ainswick Orange

There were four constables in uniform and three other men in suits. Maggie tried to guess their rank based on the quality of their tailoring.

Lady Ainswick brought a beefy man in a well-cut suit forward. He had thinning brown hair and, as if to compensate, a large, meticulously groomed moustache.

"Professor Eliot, Lord Raynham, this is Assistant Chief Constable Murphy. Assistant Chief Constable, may I present Lord Raynham and Professor Eliot. Professor Eliot and Mrs Brooks found poor Mr Mitchell."

Assistant Chief Constable Murphy looked like the last thing he wanted was to meet someone else with a title who would present issues of both county politics and protocol. But he shook hands anyhow.

"Yes. Very well. Now, Lady Ainswick, my men will need to secure the crime scene. The pathologist should be arriving shortly, as well as the SOCOs, our forensics people. If you would please wait in the house, Detective Inspector Grey will want to take everyone's statement in due course."

"And the Ainswick Orange?" Lady Ainswick asked anxiously.

"What? Oh, your little plant? Yes, we will see if there is any sign of it."

Lord Raynham spoke up. "I know it may seem trivial to you, Assistant Chief Constable, especially compared to a murder, but the little plant, as you call it, is worth a fortune to Rochford Manor. Some might say it is priceless."

Murphy tried to cover his irritation with a reassuring smile. "Of course. I understand your concern. You can count on our best efforts."

One of the other men, who introduced himself as Detective Sergeant Hilliard, came to escort the civilians back to the house, while the constables started putting up police tape.

"Please watch where you step!" Lady Ainswick cautioned. "Some of these plants are worth hundreds of pounds. Please do be careful!"

Murphy gave a short bark of laughter and quickly tried to compose himself. "Constables, you heard Lady Ainswick. Try not to step on the plants."

Geoff walked back towards the house with Lady Ainswick, and Lord Raynham with Maggie, accompanied by Sergeant Hilliard.

"I'm afraid the police are not taking your and Lady Ainswick's concerns about the snowdrop very seriously," Maggie remarked.

"Indeed."

"It would be different, I suppose, if it had been a famous painting or a fifty-carat diamond that had been stolen."

"In either of those cases, the police would doubtless avail themselves of experts from Scotland Yard, who would know which criminals specialise in stealing art or jewellery and where such thieves would try to dispose of a Monet or the Koh-I-Noor."

"You mean there are no Galanthus Pink Panthers or fences for snowdrops?"

"At least not yet. And that's assuming the Ainswick Orange was taken for its monetary value. If it were stolen because someone wanted the Ainswick Orange for himself..."

"One of your collectors, do you mean?"

"Quite."

"So we're back to Rottweilers again."

Lord Raynham smiled grimly.

"Or wait. Even better. Landmines."

"Landmines might be a bit extreme."

"I'm not sure Lady Ainswick would agree with you right now."

"The murder coupled with the theft has certainly been a shock."

"And this comes on top of Lord Ainswick's heart attack and the return of the reprehensible Edward," Maggie thought.

Aloud she asked, "You don't think Edward Symeon could be involved, do you?"

"I certainly hope not. Although Edward's aversion to snowdrops is well known. In fact he's been heard to say that when he inherits, he intends to plough under every last flower at Rochford Manor. However, his previous, er, offenses all involved people, not property."

Maggie was shocked. "Destroy the gardens? He wouldn't really, would he? Surely there must be some way to prevent that."

"I'm sure the Ainswicks are considering their options. But Edward is a terrible person. I would never underestimate what he might be capable of. And you should keep that in mind if you ever have any contact with him. As long as he's around."

Chapter Seven. Titania

'Titania' is of one the Greatorex doubles, bred by Hector Greatorex, a commissioned cavalry officer in World War I and a captain of the Home Guard in World War II. Later he became a recluse and lived in a converted railway carriage at the bottom of his garden in Brundall, Norfolk. He crossed Galanthus nivalis 'flore pleno' with Galanthus plicatus, which resulted in a range of tall and vigorous hybrid doubles. He named the plants after characters from Shakespeare's plays.

In Shakespeare's Midsummer Night's Dream, Titania is the Queen of the Fairies. G. 'Titania' is an outstanding, regularly-flowered hemispherical double that seldom displays aberrant segments. It has narrow and widely-splayed foliage with stems of up to eight inches tall.

The group reached the Study House and Lady Ainswick turned to Maggie and Lord Raynham.

"Given there are quite a number of us, I thought it would be better to gather everyone here," she explained.

Inside Maggie found Chloe and Charlotte in charge of the refreshment table and all the weekend's attendees standing together in small groups.

Maggie saw Anne talking with Derek and Damien in a far corner. She went over to check on her friend.

"The police have arrived," she announced.

"So I gather," said Anne.

"A SOCO unit is coming. And the pathologist."

Derek suddenly broke into song in a cracked falsetto. "As Coroner I must aver, I thoroughly examined her. And she's not only merely dead, she's really most sincerely dead."

Damien clapped a hand over Derek's mouth. "Sorry. It's the stress."

"*Wizard of Oz*. 'Ding Dong the Witch is Dead,'" explained Derek, putting into words what everyone had been hesitant to say.

"If Mitch hadn't been murdered, I would say he was the most likely suspect for the theft. But someone else must have also been after the snowdrop. And either got there first and was discovered by Mitch and killed him, or discovered Mitch stealing the snowdrop and killed him," Damien theorised.

"I think Mitch had come to steal the snowdrop and got killed by a second thief and the killer took the snowdrop. Mitch was hit from behind and his trowel had no dirt on it," Maggie said.

"My dear, we bow to your superior knowledge of the crime scene," said Damien.

"And better you than me," added Derek.

"And now the police are going to want to check our alibis," said Anne.

"For what time? When was Mitch murdered?" demanded Derek.

"It must have been light already. Mitch didn't have a flashlight. And finding a single plant in the dark even with a flashlight would have been near impossible. And a light might have been noticed," Anne replied.

"And we found his body a little after nine o'clock, so it had to have been before then," Maggie added.

"Well Derek and I are each other's alibi. We've been together the whole time since dinner last night. Showered, got dressed, ate breakfast, then here."

"What about when one of you was in the shower. The other could have slipped out," argued Anne.

"Not enough time," said Damien. "We've trained ourselves to take three minute showers."

"Sometimes three minutes showers together," teased Derek.

"Save the planet," said Damien.

"So you're in the clear. Even though someone is bound to mention Mitch's remarks at dinner," added Anne.

"Sticks and stones," shrugged Damien.

While Maggie remembered what she had overheard the previous night, she decided not to say anything. People frequently used hyperbole when they were upset and said things they didn't really mean, didn't they?

"How about you girls?" asked Derek.

"We went to the dining room looking for coffee as soon as we could. I arrived a few minutes before Maggie. 7:30 I think?" Anne turned to Maggie, who nodded.

"We had breakfast, got ready and then drove over here and walked around. That's when we found the body."

"So it looks like we've all got alibis," said Damien, looking relieved.

"Although you know, not to be a party pooper, but they say the police are always suspicious of the person who finds the body. And you remember Inspector Morse's law. 'There's a fifty-fifty chance that whoever finds the body, did the deed,'" Derek added.

Damien punched Derek on the arm. "Really, Derek."

"Well, it's true!"

"Don't forget that the police are also suspicious of convenient alibis," said Anne.

"But what's our motive?" asked Derek. "If the murder was about the snowdrop, someone who knew about it must have planned to take it. Mitch heard about it in London, so he said. We only heard about it last night."

"And what would we do with it?" added Damien. "We're not collectors who would hide it away in some back corner of our garden and gloat about having it. And we're not in competition with Rochford Manor. We're here because our clients keep asking about snowdrops. And it's not like we'd get anything out of hurting the Ainswicks' business. In fact, they're one of our suppliers."

"Okay, okay, you guys are in the clear," Anne laughed, while Maggie said nothing.

"As long as the police think like you do," said Derek.

"And they're not homophobes," added Damien.

Maggie looked shocked and Derek noticed.

"You're in the country here, Maggie, and everything is not up to date in Kansas City, if I can quote another show tune."

"But certainly there'd need to be some evidence," said Maggie.

"Well, it would be convenient if they found some of Professor Wolford's white hairs on the corpse or the Ainswick Orange stuffed in Violet Ashbury's make-up case. But that's pretty unlikely," said Derek.

"And don't forget, it could be a complete stranger. Someone none of us knows. We're not the only people who come to Rochford Manor. And Mitch said he heard about it in London. Other people could have heard as well," offered Damien.

"The plant world is a hotbed of gossip and intrigue," agreed Derek.

The outside door banged open and Edward Symeon walked in, wearing the same pants and jacket as the night before, but with a yellow shirt this time.

"So I hear we've had a little misadventure," he said to the room at large.

"Is Mother here? They said at the house she was here. Mother? Chloe?" he called out.

There was complete silence. Then Geoff walked over to Edward and spoke to him quietly. He and Edward went through the door behind the screen, and Maggie heard Edward say, "What the hell is going on, Mother?" before the door closed.

"Well, he and Mitch certainly make a matched set," said Damien.

"Finalists in the category for Most Obnoxious," agreed Derek.

"I wonder whether Edward has an alibi," said Anne.

"Oh I really hope he does," said Maggie.

As the others looked at her in surprise, she clarified. "It would be terrible for the Ainswicks if he were involved."

"That's true," agreed Anne.

Detective Sergeant Hilliard and Detective Inspector Grey entered and everyone stopped talking. The Sergeant was tall and thin, while the inspector was shorter and stouter than his younger colleague.

"Laurel and Hardy," thought Maggie, remembering the comedic duo from the 1930's and 40's.

"So you are not inconvenienced any longer than necessary, we would like to interview each of you individually to get any information you can provide. Please come with Detective Sergeant Hilliard when he calls your name," announced the inspector.

"How very, what? Inspector Morse again?" said Anne.

"We can only hope he's that good," said Damien gloomily.

"Mrs Brooks," intoned Sergeant Hilliard.

Anne rolled her eyes at Maggie and strode off with the sergeant. In half an hour, she had returned.

"How was it?" Maggie just had time to ask before her name was called.

"Mrs Eliot?"

Maggie stood.

"Come with me, if you please."

The sergeant was polite. He led Maggie through a door in the muralled wall, down a short hall and into a room that apparently served as a small office. Inspector Grey sat behind a battered wooden desk on which stood a computer screen and an in-box full of neatly stacked papers. A bookcase held file boxes. A chair from the lecture room had been placed in front of the desk. The inspector gestured to Maggie that she should sit, which she did.

Inspector Grey seemed to be reviewing notes he had taken on a pad. He had a round face, thinning brown hair and a neatly trimmed moustache. The sergeant, long faced, with ash blonde hair cut short, stood beside him.

"Mrs Eliot?"

"No."

"But it is Eliot, isn't it? Miss Eliot? Ms?" The inspector scowled.

"It's Professor Eliot."

"What kind of professor?"

"Social sciences."

"That so? Where?"

"Oxford."

"Oxford. That's just wonderful." He glowered, as though she had become another of his problems.

Remembering the various references to Inspector Morse, Maggie recalled that the police in the detective series frequently disliked Oxford professors, who were usually portrayed as unpleasant, condescending and duplicitous. And also that, all too often, the professor, and not the butler, was the one who "did it."

"And you're here because…"

"I'm here for the snowdrop study weekend."

"You like flowers, huh?"

Maggie decided the question was rhetorical and remained silent. The inspector scowled even more, if that were possible. Maggie decided he would soon need Botox if he continued this way. Perhaps Sylvia could recommend someone.

"So you discovered the body of Mr Mitchell."

"Yes."

"With Mrs Brooks."

"Yes."

"And how did it happen that you were in that part of the estate? I understand the lectures take place here."

"Yesterday Lady Ainswick had said that we could explore the grounds if we happened to have some free time. So we did. We were walking around and came upon Mr Mitchell."

"The area where you found him is fairly off the beaten track, isn't it."

"It was an area we had not seen as yet."

The inspector frowned some more.

"So what were you doing before you arrived at Rochford Manor and found Mr Mitchell?"

"I am staying at the Rochford Inn. I got up around 6:30, got dressed and joined Mrs Brooks for breakfast at 7:30. By about 8:30 Mrs Brooks and I were ready, so we decided to come here. The first lecture wasn't to start until 9:30."

The inspector consulted his notes.

"Humpf," he went. Maggie guessed her story matched Anne's.

"How well did you know Mr Mitchell?"

"I had only met him for the first time yesterday."

"You're both Americans," he suggested.

"Yes," said Maggie.

He waited for her to expand and then, when she remained silent, asked, "What did you think of him?"

Inspector Grey reminded Maggie of one of her department chairs when she was just beginning her academic career as an assistant professor. The man had been sexist and a bully and she remembered her strategy for dealing with him. "Charm and disarm."

However, Maggie was no longer a mere assistant professor. So she sat back in her chair and crossed her legs. They were long and elegant, even in her trousers.

"Very Sharon Stone in *Basic Instinct*. Except I'm wearing underwear," she told herself.

Aloud she said, "He was rude and obnoxious. Possibly had a drinking problem. I found him pathetic, really."

The inspector stared at her, then said, "So you admit you disliked him?"

"Inspector Grey, as far as I can tell, everyone disliked him. But if I did away with every asshole I ever encountered, the world would no longer have a population problem."

The inspector spluttered and his sergeant tried to hide a smile. Grey looked at his notes.

"When you found the body, what did you do?"

"Since it was obvious that he was dead, we, Mrs Brooks and I, knew not to disturb the scene, I guess you'd call it. There was no mobile phone reception, so Mrs Brooks went back to the Manor to call the police and I stayed to make sure no one else went near the body."

"Brave of you."

Maggie shrugged.

"And did anyone come along?"

Maggie hesitated. "Yes. A child. She said her name was Emily. The daughter of Charlotte Verney, Lady Ainswick's niece."

"And what did she do?"

"Nothing. I sent her away to find her mother."

"And after that?"

THE AINSWICK ORANGE

"Lady Ainswick came with Mrs Brooks, Mr Mortimer and Lord Raynham. Lady Ainswick was upset by what she saw and fainted, so Mrs Brooks and Mr Mortimer took her back to the house, while Lord Raynham and I stayed with the body to await your arrival."

The inspector regarded her, his eyes moving up her legs to her face. "You're tall for a woman, Professor Eliot. Mr Mitchell was also quite tall. Whoever hit him with that rock had to be near his height."

Maggie sighed. She didn't know if the inspector were good at his job or not, although she assumed he would have to be if he were assigned to a case like this one. But she was not going to rise to his bait.

"No, not necessarily, Inspector. If Mr Mitchell were there to steal the Ainswick Orange, he would have been squatting, or kneeling, and anyone could have come from behind and smashed in his skull with that rock."

"That's your opinion."

"That's my opinion, but it is based on observation. I spent quite a bit of time waiting at the scene. I was probably there longer than you were."

"Enough time so you could have altered…"

Maggie interrupted. "Could have, perhaps, but I did not, and as I did not, you will certainly not find anything which would indicate that I did."

They glared at each other.

"And how did you know about this plant, this Ainswick Orange?"

Maggie decided not to mention Lord Raynham. "Mitch, Mr Mitchell, mentioned it last night. He said he had heard rumours about it in London and asked Lady Ainswick if they were true. She replied that it was not her policy to comment on rumour. The discussion ended there."

"And what was his reaction?"

"He pouted. It was in character."

"Did he get into any arguments with anyone else?"

"Like I said, he was an asshole. So yes, he was obnoxious, but I didn't hear anything that would provoke someone to murder him. Unless disliking ornamental grasses provided a motive."

The inspector sat quietly with his lips pursed together while he leafed through his notes.

"Very well, Professor Eliot. That's all my questions for now. But stick around. I may have more later."

Chapter Eight. Carolyn Elwes

Galanthus elwesii 'Carolyn Elwes' is named after Lady Elwes of Colesbourne Park, in Gloucestershire.

Lady Elwes was urged to take an interest in the snowdrops at Colesbourne by her cousin, Mary Biddulph of Rodmarton Manor, which is also famous for its snowdrops. She introduced her to Richard Nutt, gardener to the Mathias' of The Giant Snowdrop Company. Nutt helped identify the surviving Galanthus which had originally been brought back from Turkey to Colesbourne by Henry John Elwes in 1874. Discoveries at Colesbourne since then include the early G. plicatus Colossus, G. elwesii George Elwes and G. Lord Lieutenant.

'Carolyn Elwes' is the first yellow elwesii. It has three narrow, upright, yellow-tipped leaves, while the spathe and inner markings are also yellow. The colour becomes more pronounced when the snowdrop is grown in the sun. Introduced in 1993, most of the plants were stolen in 1997 and have never been recovered. It has only recently been offered to galanthophiles again.

One by one, people were called for interviews. Time dragged by. At noon, Lady Ainswick and Charlotte came in with platters of sandwiches, bowls of salads and dishes of apple crumble with accompanying custard sauce.

Lady Ainswick explained. "Since we are not permitted to go to the inn for lunch, the Markhams have kindly provided us with some food. Please help yourselves."

Maggie took the opportunity to talk to Charlotte. "Hi. I'm Maggie Eliot. Is Emily your daughter?"

Charlotte nodded.

"Is she all right? It was pretty gruesome. Nothing you'd want a young girl to see."

"I think she's all right. She seemed to be. I'll ask her again later. She's at the house with Chloe."

"That's good. I just wanted to make sure."

"Thank you. I appreciate that you're concerned."

The group devoured the food, both as a reaction to the stress of the situation and because it was something to do to relieve the tedium.

Maggie ate a sandwich, then looked around. Violet and Sylvia were sitting together. Both had taken salad and bits of lettuce still remained on their plates. From Maggie's vantage point, it looked like Sylvia was showing Violet something pertaining to her manicure. Violet was nodding.

In another corner, Geoff sat with Professor Wolford and the Townsends. Maggie could just hear the Townsends, who were asking the experts what they thought about their ideas to expand their snowdrop collection and if the soil and growing conditions at their Devon property would support their plans.

From time to time, Maggie saw Geoff glance wistfully across at Sylvia, but Sylvia ignored him. Once the woman noticed his look, frowned to the extent her Botox would allow and turned away.

Their behaviour reminded Maggie of certain of her students the last time she had taught a freshman introductory course. Their link ups and break ups had absorbed much more of their attention than anything she had to say about the consequences of US immigration policy.

The Puseys were keeping to themselves, but Maggie saw that Sarah would also look at Geoff and then at Sylvia, like a spectator at a tennis match. As Sylvia continued to disregard the plantsman and he became increasingly morose, Sarah smiled slyly, as though she knew some secret. Remembering what she had heard the previous evening, Maggie wondered if perhaps she did.

Maggie was still sitting with Anne, Derek and Damien, who were discussing a play they had all seen in London the previous fall. Maggie looked around for Lord Raynham, but he was not in the room. Since he had been asked to remain like the rest of them, she assumed he must be behind the scenes with Lady Ainswick and Charlotte. There was no sign of the prodigal Edward.

By 1:30, Maggie decided she needed to use the WC, which was down the hall from the office the police were using. On her return, the door to the room was slightly ajar and she could hear voices. She crept forward as quietly as she could and stopped just outside.

Inspector Grey was saying, "So that's the lot of them. All of them can account for themselves, and even the ones with no one to back them up, well, where else are they going to be except in bed at seven bloody o'clock on a Saturday morning?

"None of them liked the bloke, they all thought he was a right wanker, but none of them seem to have a real reason to kill him. And tomorrow they'd have all been off and never had to see him again. So that leaves the friggin' flower. Did any of these people steal it and kill Mitchell in the process? I have no evidence and I'll need evidence if I'm to get in to search their rooms."

"Maybe the SOCOs will find something. Or the pathologist."

Maggie heard a noise and turned to see Lady Ainswick come around the corner. Maggie put her finger to her lips and motioned to the woman to come forward quietly. Maggie took her arm and indicated she should listen as well.

"Someone in the family could have done him if they caught him stealing. But then why take the snowdrop? Why not just leave it there? But that son is a bad 'un for sure."

"And he has no alibi," Hilliard pointed out.

"And then there's that baron fellow."

"What about him, sir?"

"You wouldn't remember, you weren't even born yet, but when I was a lad, there was a suspicious death at that place of his. Beaumatin. It was his older brother. The heir. Tumbled down the stairs and broke his neck. So the younger brother inherited. My uncle George was on the force at the time. He's the reason I became a copper, you know?

"Anyhow, Uncle George was the lead inspector and I know he fancied Raynham for it, but there was no proof. So he was never charged. It haunted Uncle George until the day he died, having to let a murderer get away with it. And you know what they say about the second murder being easier than the first."

The inspector was pensive. "And he's got no alibi."

"But he's got no motive either, sir," Sergeant Hilliard pointed out.

THE AINSWICK ORANGE

The inspector considered this. "He's very tight with the Ainswicks. Maybe he found Mitchell trying to steal this bloody plant, got into a struggle, killed him and took it himself to throw us off the scent. Make it look like it was one thief surprised by another."

"Or maybe he just wanted it for himself, sir. They say he's got a garden full of those snowdrops."

"Maybe. These people with their titles and money. They always think the rules don't apply."

Grey sighed.

"Or maybe it was just someone off the street we don't even know about. They've had thieves stealing these things here before. Silly little flowers. Some worth hundreds of pounds, they tell me. People've got more money than sense."

"That's for certain, sir."

"Meanwhile we're stuck in some Agatha Christie whodunit with lords and ladies and black sheep sons and society bitches and snooty professors and nancy boys. I'd like to arrest the lot of them on suspicion of impersonating a detective story."

"We've got our work cut out for us, sir," agreed his sycophantic sergeant.

Maggie heard Grey push back his chair. She turned to Lady Ainswick, who pulled her down the hall and out of sight around the corner. They heard the policemen close the door and walk off in the other direction.

"Well!" said Lady Ainswick.

She and Maggie looked at each other. "What do you think?"

"I think that unless some compelling evidence turns up, we can't rely on Inspector Grey to overcome his prejudices and preconceptions and uncover Mitch's murderer, let alone find the Ainswick Orange," said Maggie.

"So what do we do?" Lady Ainswick was obviously distressed.

"We're going to do exactly what we would do if we were in an Agatha Christie story. Try to figure it out ourselves. Inspector Grey says we can't leave, so we can observe. Listen to people talk to each other. Watch how they interact. My friend Anne, Mrs Brooks, is an expert judge of character. She has had to be to navigate the shoals of Oxford academic life for thirty years. Let's see what we can find out. Who can be eliminated, who is suspicious."

"I can't believe anyone here would kill someone."

"I agree. But it's said that, given the right circumstances, anyone could commit a murder."

"And if it's some random poacher?"

"That would be a job for the police."

Maggie paused, then asked. "You don't have any security? Cameras? Gates?"

"No. We've never really needed any before, until recently. And the idea of cameras… So distasteful. Lord Raynham says you told him he should get Rottweilers."

Maggie was surprised. But also pleased. "Rottweilers would be good. You wouldn't have to worry about poachers, anyway."

"So what do you think we should do?"

"As long as we have to remain here, why not continue with the programme. I think Geoff was going to speak about yellow snowdrops? And then the dinner and the auction. If it is too much for Lord Ainswick, perhaps we could hold it at the inn. It would be an excellent opportunity for observation."

"Keep calm and carry on, then?" said Lady Ainswick. "Excellent advice. We think alike, I see."

Charlotte appeared. "Aunt Beatrix? Oh, here you are. Inspector Grey wants to see all of us in the lecture room."

Lady Ainswick led Maggie into a kitchen, where there was the unexpected sight of Chloe washing tea cups and Lord Raynham drying them with a chequered tea towel.

"The inspector would like to see us in the Study Hall," Lady Ainswick announced.

They trooped out through the door into the main room. Maggie felt Lord Raynham standing close behind her. Uncomfortably close. Close enough so that she could feel the warmth from his body in the otherwise cool room.

"Get a grip, Eliot!" she told herself. "All the man has done is make some casual conversation. He's being polite, is all."

"How did it go with the fuzz?" he asked quietly.

"They think I'm a snooty professor and are disappointed that Anne and I can alibi each other. On the basis that it would make it easy for them if the one who discovered the body was also the guilty party. How about you?"

"As I have no alibi and the inspector still harbours suspicions from forty years ago, I am apparently a prime suspect," he said.

"You're joking!" said Maggie, although she had heard the inspector say so himself.

"No, unfortunately, I'm not."

Maggie would have said more, but the inspector cleared his throat to get the group's attention.

"I want to thank you all for your cooperation. While we await the initial reports from the pathologist's examination and forensics, I would like to request that everyone remain available in Rochford in case additional questions arise."

"And when do you expect those reports?" It was Lady Ainswick.

"Hopefully by tomorrow."

"Very well."

The policemen went out. After the door had closed, Lady Ainswick addressed the group.

"Since everyone has been asked to remain, I suggest we continue with the lectures and with the dinner and auction tonight. And we will donate a portion of the auction proceeds to a local charity in Mr Mitchell's name."

"I'm sure Mitch would have loved that," murmured Maggie.

"Lady Ainswick has always had an unfailing appreciation of the ironic," replied Lord Raynham.

"Everyone please sort yourselves and we will start in…" Lady Ainswick consulted her watch. "Fifteen minutes."

The Ainswick Orange

Violet and the Puseys went outside to smoke. Maggie decided she would like to get some fresh air before having to sit through more slides of what to her seemed to be identical Galanthus. She walked around in the formal gardens behind the house for some minutes, peeked in the greenhouse windows where hundreds of snowdrops stood on shelves in pots, ready for sale, and then headed back to the lecture hall. George Pusey and Violet had gone back inside, but Sarah Pusey was still working on her cigarette.

Maggie smiled at her and commented, "Not exactly the weekend we signed up for."

Sarah inhaled and shrugged.

From around the corner of the building, Maggie heard a female hiss, "Well, you've got it, don't you? You haven't fucked that up too?"

A male voice mumbled a response.

Maggie, who was nearer to the speaker, glanced at Sarah to see if she had heard as well, but the woman seemed absorbed in getting her nicotine fix.

Then around the corner stalked Sylvia Biddle-Pew, who came to an abrupt halt when she saw the two women. She nodded at Maggie and then continued her catwalk strut into the building.

Moments later, Geoff came around the other corner of the building at a trot. Had he been the one to whom Sylvia had been talking? They had seemed quite chummy yesterday and there was Geoff's visit to Sylvia's room last night. Geoff could have easily gone around the Study House to avoid being seen coming from the same direction as Sylvia. Was Sylvia's ignoring Geoff an attempt to conceal a relationship from the police? Why? Maggie wondered.

Geoff also stopped short when he saw Maggie and Sarah. Then he gave an unconvincing smile and said, "Well, let's start the programme, shall we?"

Geoff followed the women into the building. Sarah joined George and the Townsends, while Maggie headed to where she saw Anne standing with Derek, Damien and Lord Raynham.

As people seated themselves, Lord Raynham pulled out a chair for Maggie and took the one next to hers. She ignored Anne's wink.

Maggie began to wonder what to make of the words she had overheard. What was Geoff supposed to have? The Ainswick Orange? And what had he messed up? Being surprised by Mitch and having to resort to murder? Maggie tried to think of other ways to interpret Sylvia's remarks.

Perhaps it was something the woman considered vital to her comfort, like a goose down comforter. The inn used synthetic bed covers and blankets. Which would surely not be up to Sylvia's exacting standards. And while Sylvia's driver was carrying sheets and pillows when she checked in, Maggie did not remember a duvet. Or maybe she still blamed Geoff for not securing her lodging at the manor. With someone like Sylvia, that was a possibility,

And there was another problem. Why would Geoff take the Ainswick Orange? Surely it was more in his interest to have it at Rochford Manor. While Maggie would not put it past Sylvia to steal the plant if she wanted it or, more likely, pay someone else to steal it, why would Geoff agree? How much could she pay him that would be worth his career and his reputation if he were caught?

"Professor Eliot?" Lord Raynham interrupted her thoughts. "Professor Eliot, are you there?"

"Oh, I'm sorry. I got distracted. Something I overheard."

"About the murder?"

"Perhaps. Or perhaps about... goose down."

"What?"

Geoff had risen and turned on the projector. A clump of snowdrops with yellow ovaries appeared on the screen.

"Later," murmured Lord Raynham.

The man was sitting on Maggie's left and she had to look past him to see the screen. She was intensely aware of his nearness and she could smell his scent. It was subtle. Something with citrus and spice. Not cologne. He did not seem the type. Perhaps aftershave. Out of an old fashioned crystal bottle with a seal, "By appointment to..."

"Oh dear, this is bad," Maggie told herself. "As if someone like him would have any interest in some post-menopausal, American university professor."

Maggie had had two serious relationships before the one she and Anne referred to as "the Lying Bastard." Both were with fellow academics back in the US and, in both cases, the men had made their expectations clear that their careers would come first.

The men had also made it obvious that, while they were supportive of Maggie's working, they also assumed she would take primary responsibility for the household and any children that might be forthcoming. And even though this was basically the same arrangement that had been accepted by her other female colleagues who were married, for Maggie it was, "Thanks, but no thanks."

Maggie was startled by being nudged by Lord Raynham. She felt a jolt of electricity and was embarrassed to feel herself blushing.

"The Ainswick Orange," Lord Raynham leaned over and murmured in her ear, making her even more uncomfortable. Could he sense how she was feeling? Dear God, she hoped not. He remained close to her and her stomach started to do wobblies.

Geoff was speaking. "Lady Ainswick felt that as you are all being inconvenienced by this sad episode, we should show you what it seems to be about."

On the screen was a slide of a snowdrop. As Lord Raynham had predicted, it had an ovary of bright orange. Pure white petals hung down gracefully but inside, the inner petals were also liberally marked with the orange colour.

"The Ainswick Orange was discovered by Lord Ainswick two years ago on a visit to the nuclear reprocessing plant at Sellafield. Sellafield, you may remember, was also the site of the Windscale Nuclear Fire in 1957. Whilst no one was evacuated because of the Windscale incident, it still rates as the worst nuclear accident in Britain's history and milk from the area was destroyed for months afterward.

"Lord Ainswick was visiting as part of a commission reviewing Britain's nuclear power needs. Leaving a restaurant where the group had had dinner, he spotted the plant blooming in a embankment beside the car park. He asked the restaurant's owners if he might take it, as he was a galanthophile, and they graciously consented. He paid them £20 pounds for the plant, which they were surprised but pleased to accept. He brought the snowdrop back to Rochford Manor, where it has been carefully nurtured since.

"Yellow snowdrops have a tendency to be less hardy than other varieties and the Ainswick Orange also languished its first year here and produced no flowers. This year, however, it had three and we were optimistic that it would flourish to the point it could be reproduced. Now, however…" Geoff turned his hands palms up.

Derek raised his hand. "Do you think the colour is the result of a mutation caused by the fallout from the accident?"

"It is certainly a theory. We know that at Chernobyl there have been mutations of local flora and fauna, and now at Fukushima as well. Of course, the fallout from both Chernobyl and Fukushima was magnitudes worse than Windscale."

Daphne Townsend asked, "But the snowdrop wasn't radioactive?"

Geoff smiled. "No, although Lord Ainswick did have that checked."

"Isn't there another orange snowdrop? The Anglesey Orange Tip?" was Damien's question.

"Yes. I think I even have a slide…" Geoff flipped through his presentation. Then a picture appeared of a snowdrop with long petals whose tips were streaked with pale orange.

"Before the Ainswick Orange, the Anglesey Orange Tip was the most true-to-colour orange snowdrop to date and produced a lot of excitement at its introduction in 2010. Joy Cozens was the previous claimant to being the first orange snowdrop. Unfortunately, its dull orange takes at least two years to develop and is fleeting when it finally does appear. In comparison, the colour at the ends of the outer segments of

Anglesey Orange Tip remains evident throughout its blooming period.

"You should know that the Anglesey Orange Tip is being watched round-the-clock by security guards. We had not thought such measures were necessary."

Sarah Pusey asked, "What would such a plant be worth?"

"The Ainswick Orange? Hard to say. But it is unique. We had not reproduced it. So you could say it is priceless. Worth whatever someone would pay. Not that it is for sale. We are still years away, or we were years away, from having plants for the market."

Geoff closed the presentation and the screen went blank. "Anyhow, now you know what the Ainswick Orange looks like. So if you happen to see it, don't disturb it, but please let me know immediately."

"How would we see it?" demanded George Pusey. "I understood it was stolen."

"Yes, but I imagine whoever took it would not want to be discovered with it, given the police investigation. It is possible it is far away by now, but it is also possible it has been replanted amongst another group of snowdrops where it would not be noticed until it was safe to retrieve it."

Maggie said softly to Lord Raynham. "That's what you said."

Lord Raynham nodded.

Lady Ainswick stepped forward.

"So that is our abbreviated programme. We will meet again at the house at seven for cocktails, dinner and our auction. In the meantime, our grounds are still mostly available for you to explore. There are also some quite lovely villages in the vicinity. I am sure when Inspector Grey said not to leave, he did not mean you were prisoners. If you just stay between Cheltenham and Cirencester, I am sure it will be all right."

Lord Raynham turned to Maggie. "I have some chores to do back at Beaumatin, but I'll see you at the dinner. Are you going to join in the auction?"

"I would like to. I'd planned to get some plants to thank Mrs Brooks for bringing me. I guess I still should. It's for a good cause. Rochford Manor, I mean, not Mr Mitchell. But I certainly don't know what a particular plant would be worth and I don't want to bid foolishly."

"I'd be happy to assist with that."

"Thank you, that's very kind," Maggie smiled. Lord Raynham walked off and Maggie went and found Anne, who had gone to ask Geoff some questions.

When she had gotten her answers, Anne said, "Well I wouldn't mind taking a drive around. This is not an area I get to often. I tend to stay north of the A40. Interested?"

"Absolutely!"

So Anne and Maggie took off to drive through more picturesque small villages, reached by harrowingly narrow, winding roads. Still, it was good to get away. The morning seemed like an eternity ago and Maggie felt she could hardly remember leaving Bear the previous morning. Was it only yesterday they had arrived?

They stopped at one of the tea shops that seemed to have proliferated in the Cotswolds like kudzu in the US

South. After they both had ordered cappuccinos, Maggie told her friend what she had overheard Inspector Grey say and Lady Ainswick's and her idea about trying to identify the thief and hopefully the murderer themselves.

"Just by observing. Not by doing anything risky."

"Three Miss Marples are better than one?"

"More or less."

"Too bad Mitch is dead. If any of our group were a thief and a murderer, it should have been him."

"I'm sure he'd agree with you. About being dead, I mean."

"I know. Loathsome though he was, no one deserves to have his head bashed in."

There was a pause, then Maggie asked, "What's the story with Edward Symeon?"

"The Ainswicks' bad boy? Also definitely in the loathsome category. After years of scandals, and burning through the family fortune at an impressive rate, or as much of the fortune as he could get his hands on, he was told he wouldn't get another pence unless he agreed to leave the country.

"Some sort of trust was established to be paid into a foreign bank account of his choosing, as long as it was far enough away so the Ainswicks would no longer be embarrassed by his bad behaviour. He chose Cyprus and has been there these past ten years. Why he came back now, which is certainly against the terms of the agreement, I have no idea. I'm not sure I believe what he said about being concerned about Lord Ainswick."

THE AINSWICK ORANGE

"You did say you saw that lawyer who specialises in trusts at Rochford yesterday."

"Yes. There could be something going on. I don't know what, though. Or whether it has anything to do with Mitch's murder. And although I wouldn't put it past Symeon to filch the family silver, what would he do with a snowdrop? How would he even know of its existence?"

"Maybe he learned about it in London too. On his way to Rochford from Cyprus. I assume he'd have had to fly in through London. And that's where everyone else seems to have heard."

Anne looked startled.

"Just kidding. Or I think I'm kidding. But one thing you might know. It's about all these titles. I had a hard enough time figuring out how academic titles worked at Oxford, compared to the US. And now with these... I guess they're peers?"

They ordered two more cappuccinos from the passing waitress.

"Why is the vile Edward Edward Symeon and not Edward Ainswick? Why did Lord Raynham introduce himself as simply Raynham? Why is it Lady Ainswick and not Viscountess Ainswick and Lord Raynham, not Baron Raynham? But at dinner last night his place card read 'The Lord Raynham' and not just Lord Raynham. I'm hopelessly confused."

"I know. It's complex. And I'm no expert, I'm afraid. You'd need to look at Debrett's for that. Mainly, it's social usage. These rules. Or perhaps conventions is a better term. Like why you start with the fork furthest away from your plate rather than the one nearest. Either way has a certain logic, but only one is considered to be correct.

"Anyhow, all peers—dukes, marquises, earls, viscounts, barons—have their own family names. They had them before they were awarded with titles for services to the monarch. In whatever century. Or, once the title was established, had them before they inherited. Lord Ainswick's family name is Symeon and Lord Raynham's is Conyers, I believe. As for why it's not Viscountess Ainswick, well I guess it's similar to why at Oxford you're Professor Eliot and not Dr Eliot, like you'd be in the US."

"And why isn't Chloe Symeon Lady Chloe, like Lady Crista Carrington?"

Lady Crista Carrington was the wife of Alastair Carrington, who was the Master of Merrion College.

"Lady Crista is the daughter of an earl and earl's daughters are called 'Lady.' A duke's oldest son often has his own title or titles, like viscount. And a duke himself can have more than one title. A viscount's children are referred to as "honourable" when you send them a letter, on the envelope, but otherwise are just plain Mr or Miss or Mrs.

"You can look at all up. In Debrett's or even Wikipedia. A lot of the peerage have their own pages, like the Dukes of Devonshire. They keep really careful records because of the inheritance issue. Primogeniture and all that.

"Did you know the real reason it was normal for a widow to be in mourning for a year in the old days? It was to make sure she wasn't pregnant with a possible heir, in case there wasn't a direct one already. Of course that's making the assumption that the widow was behaving herself before her husband died. In the days before paternity testing," Anne smiled.

"I know it's complicated. And then there's precedence. Who precedes whom when you go in for dinner. Who sits where. It makes lining up for an Oxford academic procession seem simple. And it's not just an ego thing. Or the social prestige. Or not only. There's property and money attached to these titles. Maybe a lot less now than before Wilson and Heath, but still enough for people to be really finicky."

Maggie shook her head.

At slightly before six, they returned to the Rochford Inn.

As Maggie got out of the car, Anne said, "Go and make yourself beautiful for your baron."

Maggie shook her head. "He's not my baron. And I thought it was lord."

Anne just laughed.

Susan Alexander

Chapter Nine. Galatea

In Greek mythology, Galatea, meaning "she who is milk white," is popularly remembered as a statue carved by Pygmalion and subsequently brought to life. The story forms the basis of an eponymous play by George Bernard Shaw and the musical My Fair Lady.

As a Galanthus, the original 'Galatea' was first mentioned by James Allen in 1891. However, it is believed that the modern version is, in fact, a different plant. It is a very early variety and can be recognised by its unusually long ovary and very long pedicel.

Hardy and easy to grow, 'Galatea' is described by Alan Street as "ticking all the boxes for a perfect snowdrop." Its similarity to the Allen clone 'Magnet' has been noted. The two can be distinguished by comparing the green inner segment markings. Both have a "V," but Galatea's "V" is a perfect right angle, whereas Magnet's "V" is no more than 70°.

Maggie dressed carefully for the evening because, as she told herself, it was not every day that she had the opportunity to dine at a viscount's ancestral home.

She had brought one dress with her to the cottage from Oxford, so that was the one she would wear that evening. It was black wool crepe with a scoop neck, long fitted sleeves and a flared skirt that had enough fullness to swirl when she walked. Anne, who had seen her wear it before, called it her "ballerina dress." Its simple lines suited her. With her height, frills and ruffles were not a good fashion choice.

She also put on one of her clandestine indulgences—high end lingerie. To offset the staid work uniforms of sweaters and trousers she habitually wore, Maggie bought fantasy lingerie to put on beneath them. No one ever knew the serious professor had on a leopard-spotted satin bra with matching bikini briefs beneath her sober black turtleneck and black gabardine pants. It gave her a sense of having a secret identity. That there was a Superman lurking beneath her workaday Clark Kent.

Maggie put on a delicate black lace bra over what she called her size "B-B" breasts, by which she meant "barely B's." She had long ago made her peace with nature and not being overly endowed had turned out to mean they were still perky at her age. She added a matching thong and sheer black stockings held up with a black lace garter belt. She wore black pumps with low heels. No Louboutin's with four-inch heels for her. Even if she didn't fall flat on her face trying to walk in them, with her height, she would look ridiculous.

Anne had given her a jar of some special gel that transformed her unruly curls to elegant ringlets, shining with coppery highlights. She held some of the curls back with a gold filigree hairclip shaped like a butterfly and let the rest fall loose. A little powder, some lip gloss and a spritz of her perfume. She grabbed her jacket and she was ready. Bring it on.

Maggie met Anne at her car just before seven. Anne, who was looking elegant in a blue knit dress and matching jacket, was also driving Derek and Damien, who had shed their country attire for some fashionable suits. They admired each other and took off.

Rochford Manor both lived up to Maggie's expectations and surprised her. Based on a few visits to some stately homes, Maggie had decided they would be horribly uncomfortable places to live, without a chair or sofa in the place where one could have curled up and read a book.

But although the interior of Rochford Manor had its share of grand architectural flourishes, it was also reassuringly homey. A pair of fluffy white bichon frises ran around, sniffing the ankles of the new arrivals, and savoury aromas of dinner cooking drifted from the back of the house.

The quartet was greeted by Lady Ainswick in a large hall with pale yellow walls and an inlaid marble floor. Half a dozen white marble busts of men who looked like Roman emperors rested on pedestals along one side, while on the other, an elegant stone staircase led to the floor above.

Lady Ainswick introduced the dogs.

"They're called Kat and Maus. Spelled K-A-T and M-A-U-S. They're short versions of their actual names, which are long and ridiculous, as these things usually are. Ainswick thinks it's funny. He's particularly attached to them and they keep him up and about with their walks."

She led them to a formal drawing room where Maggie's eyes were drawn up to an intricately plastered ceiling. Light blue walls were hung with ancestral portraits in gilded frames that were illuminated by two massive crystal chandeliers. Windows that reached from floor to ceiling were hung with brocade drapes in a blue a few shades darker than the walls.

A cheerful fire was burning in a large fireplace with an ornately carved white marble surround. Above the mantel hung a portrait of a pretty woman who wore a wonderful ivory brocade dress and whose elaborately-dressed hair was grey with powder. She sat gracefully lounging in a dainty chair with her elbow on a small table and crossed legs that revealed delicate ivory satin shoes.

"Could it actually be a Gainsborough?" Maggie wondered.

Lady Ainswick introduced her and Anne to the viscount himself. In his mid-seventies, Lord Ainswick stood straight with distinguished features, a full mane of white hair and no appearance of being someone who had recently suffered from a heart problem. Chloe was also there, in charge of serving drinks. Maggie wondered if Charlotte were on duty as well or if she were with Emily at home, wherever that was.

Maggie and Anne were offered, and accepted, glasses of champagne. Maggie noticed Sylvia and Violet had also abandoned the hard stuff for the bubbly. Both women were beautifully dressed, Violet in her favoured red wool and Sylvia in grey silk. Between them, the pair would have made a jewel heist even more profitable than a rare snowdrop's. The Townsends and Professor Wolford were also there, with the Professor enjoying his habitual sherry.

The Puseys walked in. George wore his grey suit, still in need of pressing but appropriate. Sarah, however, was wearing a tight, silver-sequined mini dress, more suitable to a night of urban clubbing than dinner at the Manor, and silver platform shoes with five-inch heels. Maggie winced for her, but as Sarah surveyed the group, she seemed self-confident.

"She must think we're a bunch of stodgy old fogeys," Maggie concluded. "And perhaps we are."

Lord Raynham was the last to arrive. He was wearing a dark blue suit of impeccable design and fit that reminded Maggie, not for the first time, that there are few sights more impressive than an Englishman who employed a first-rate tailor.

"David Beckham in his knickers notwithstanding, this is my kind of eye candy," Maggie decided.

Not forgetting her mission, Maggie eavesdropped on Lady Ainswick, who was talking to the Puseys. George, it seemed, owned a specialty printing business in Birmingham. He'd been married to Sarah for just over a year and had hopes they would soon be starting a family.

Sarah scowled at the suggestion, however, and Maggie wondered again why they had come. Sarah did not seem as though she would be interested in planting a snowdrop garden while she nursed an infant. On the other hand, that also made the Puseys unlikely snowdrop thieves.

Anne was chatting with the Townsends and Derek and Damien were entertaining Sylvia and Violet. Maggie guessed Violet could be considered a potential customer. She noticed Geoff off by the fireplace looking longingly at Sylvia, who continued to ignore him.

While Maggie privately thought the woman was a strange object for Geoff's affections, she reminded herself that she was in no position to judge. She joined Geoff after getting a refill from Chloe.

"I've been enjoying your lectures. I came only knowing 'small white flower' and I now know how to tell the difference between an elwesii and a plicatus. Or at least I think I know the difference."

"It's a specialty, in the same way you academics have specialities, with arcane knowledge and an esoteric vocabulary."

"I've been wondering about getting some of your snowdrops for my mother, but I heard Mr Mitchell say you can't import British snowdrops into the US."

Geoff made a face at the mention of the dead man. "It's a matter of having the correct authorisations and having the customs forms properly filled out. It's not impossible if you know what you're doing. But few people do. Or take the time and trouble to find out what the rules are. They try to smuggle them in and the bulbs get confiscated. I understand the New York Botanical Garden has a whole collection of rare snowdrops seized by customs and then passed on for planting."

"Well at least the public gets to benefit and they don't end up hidden away in some collector's garden. I certainly hope that's not what will happen to the Ainswick Orange."

Geoff was silent.

Maggie said casually, "Speaking of collectors, I heard Sylvia Biddle-Pew say she's one. That she already has close to one hundred varieties and that on this trip she hopes to bring back at least twenty more."

"Yes, she mentioned that to me as well."

"The Philadelphia climate, it's not a lot like here, is it? Brutally hot, humid summers. Bitterly cold winters. How do snowdrops do there?"

"There are issues, but snowdrops are fairly adaptable. Their native climate in the eastern Mediterranean gets extremes of temperatures as well."

"Does she have her own garden staff, do you know?" Geoff took a step backwards at this question, so Maggie hurried on.

"Anne Brooks occasionally plants the odd daffodil bulb, but give her a rose bush and she's on the phone to Derek and Damien to send someone over. I would assume Sylvia is the same. As well as Violet Ashbury. It's difficult to imagine

Sylvia on her knees wielding a trowel. Hard on the manicure, I imagine."

Geoff relaxed a bit. "She has a large property south of Philadelphia. Quite a few acres. Horses as well. So I would assume she has staff."

Maggie digested the extent of Geoff's knowledge. It would be like Sylvia to talk about her estate, so his having the information might not mean anything. On the other hand, given his late night visit to her room and Sylvia's welcome, she assumed theirs was more than a casual relationship. Well, better move on.

Professor Wolford was approaching Geoff, doubtless for some shop talk. Maggie walked away and came to rest in a chair at angles to the sofa where Sylvia and Violet were sitting and looking somewhat bored.

"Well this has been a day," began Maggie. "A murder. I can hardly believe it. It still seems more like a TV show. And that policeman, the inspector? Do you really think he's up for the job?"

Sylvia perked up. "A horrible man. Awful. He was positively rude when he questioned me. He obviously has no idea who I am. And when it turned out I had no alibi—well at that ungodly hour I was in my room doing my face and you girls know what that takes at our age—he seemed to find that suspicious. Suspicious! Moi?"

Violet, who had looked affronted by Sylvia's remark about her age, brightened at a chance to join in abusing the inspector.

"The same for me. Of course I was also in my room. It's not like I would eat that 'English breakfast' the inn offers. I only ever have hot water with lemon in the morning. But

Grey seemed to think I was hiding something. Now what would I have to hide? And he became quite aggressive about it. These police. They really need to be taught their place."

"Good luck with that," said Sylvia wryly.

Sylvia turned to Maggie. "You found the body. What do you think? Any ideas about who did it?"

Maggie was not about to mention what she had overheard Sylvia saying earlier. Or that she had seen Geoff visiting her room the previous night. So she responded, "No idea at all. And the grounds are open. There's no security. It could have been anyone. Apparently the Ainswicks have lost plants to poachers before."

Sylvia nodded.

"And, although I know one isn't supposed to speak ill of the dead, well, I imagine Mitch might have enemies that have nothing to do with Rochford Manor or the snowdrop weekend."

"I wonder if Inspector Grey has considered that. Probably not. He's such a small-minded little man," said Violet.

Maggie asked, "Any ideas yourself?"

Sylvia thought about this. "My first choice would have been Mitch. At least as the thief."

"I think everyone's would have been," agreed Maggie.

"And he knew about the Ainswick Orange. I wonder how he found out. He said he heard about it in London," Violet pointed out.

"And he asked about it at dinner last night. And he certainly seemed to be the only one who knew about it in our group. Expect of course for the Ainswicks. And Geoff Mortimer," Maggie added.

"And then there's the Ainswick son," Sylvia continued. "Born-to-be-wild bad boy that he is. I haven't seen him since this morning. Have you?"

Both Maggie and Violet shook their heads.

"I just hope he doesn't make an appearance tonight," said Violet.

"From what I understand, he hates snowdrops and the Rochford Manor gardens. So he probably wouldn't be interested in the auction," said Maggie.

"You can say that again," said Sylvia. "I heard he's promised to plough it all under when he inherits."

"Really? How dreadful," said Violet, while Maggie wondered how Sylvia knew this. From Geoff, perhaps?

Violet shuddered. "Finding a body. How gruesome. What did he look like?"

Maggie tried not to think about her father's stuffed fish. "He'd been hit on the head. He looked, well, dead. Like something you'd see on a TV crime show. Except it wasn't. On TV."

Sylvia drained her glass. "Nice champagne. Not vintage, but not bad. And properly chilled for a change."

She lifted the glass and turned it in the light. "Nice crystal too."

Sylvia stood. "Well, I could use some more. What about you girls?"

Maggie declined but Violet also drained her glass and handed it to Sylvia.

"Yeth pleath," she lisped, trying for cuteness but failing.

Maggie watched Sylvia head towards the table where Chloe was serving drinks, only to be intercepted by Sarah Pusey.

"Now that's strange," Maggie thought.

Sarah put her hand on Sylvia's arm and spoke rapidly in a low voice. Sylvia recoiled. Sarah continued to talk. Finally Sylvia pulled back and yanked her arm away. She continued towards Chloe, her face a frozen mask, while Sarah minced back to George in her heels.

"Please excuse me," said Maggie to Violet. She rose from her chair, turned and bumped into Lord Raynham.

"Oh! I'm so sorry," she said, flustered.

Lord Raynham smiled and looked her over. Maggie felt panic and wondered for a brief instant if he could see through her dress to her underwear.

"But that's ridiculous. Get a grip, Eliot," she told herself sternly.

Lord Raynham took her elbow and led her away to a quiet area off to the side of the room. From the corner of her eye, Maggie saw Violet give her what her mother would have called "a dirty look."

"What did you do during the break?" he asked.

"Anne and I took a drive and saw some of your lovely villages. I can't believe I've been in Oxford for eight years and never visited the Cotswolds. It's quite beautiful. Of course I must confess to being a bit less enthusiastic about your roads. If you can call them roads. Them I find quite daunting."

"Oh, you get used to them. It's mainly a question of technique. And of course having four-wheel drive helps when there's ice or mud."

"I'd imagine it would be a requirement."

"And nothing more has been seen of our good inspector and his loyal sergeant?"

"Not to my knowledge."

"Well let's hope they're off to their pub and enjoying a pint."

He said this with a hint of bitterness and Maggie looked at him with surprise.

"Sorry. This business… seems to have stirred up some memories I thought had been buried long ago."

They stood in awkward silence. Lord Raynham looked down at their glasses and noticed they were empty. He took Maggie's and went off for refills. Maggie tried to keep her mind blank by staring at a portrait on the wall of a stout man wearing an elaborate wig.

Lord Raynham returned with more champagne and raised his glass. "Well, Professor Eliot."

"Well, Lord Raynham," responded Maggie, lifting hers in return.

"Please, call me Thomas."

"If you'll drop the Professor Eliot."

"Then it's Margaret?"

"Margaret was one of my mother's aunts. A terrifying woman. She died at the age of 98, choking on some toast while she was reprimanding her maid because she felt the tea had not been brewed properly. So it's Maggie."

"Very well. Maggie, then. Tell me. What are these controversial views of yours? The quote I read said, 'When they put up Christmas trees in Riyadh, I'll put up with niqabs in Kensington."

"Oh dear. That was in *The Guardian*. I'm afraid they don't appreciate my positions and enjoy taking them out of context. I certainly don't want the notoriety.

"So my views? I'll try to give you the short version. In the late 1960's and early 70's, in the era of civil rights and feminism and the anti-Viet Nam war movement, there was a general reaction against the dominance of the 'dead white men' of western civilisation and an embracing of, I guess you would call it, cultural relativism. All cultures had equal value and deserved respect and inclusion."

"I remember."

"And that was indeed a much needed swing of the pendulum. But as usual, as these things go, the pendulum may have swung too far.

"My work focuses on immigration and cultural integration. I believe that if you immigrate in search of a better life, one of the requirements is to adapt to the culture and social values of your new homeland. Learn the language. Send your children to the local schools. And if you are not prepared to do that, you should stay where you are. Of course I'm not talking about not enjoying your native food or music, but my work supports the benefits of fitting in to your new environment.

"But I have seen honour killings in Bradford. And female genital mutilation in Portsmouth. And teenage boys tortured for being witches in London. And child brides of nine in Birmingham. These things are wrong anywhere. That they occur in Britain represents failures in immigration policy and issues with integration.

"As for burqas and niqabs, well, the French and Belgians and Dutch have it right. They should be banned. The attitudes towards women they represent…"

She stopped herself. "I'm sorry. Once I get started, I do tend to go on."

Thomas stared at her.

"You must have a very poor opinion of people who spend their time obsessed with small white flowers. You must find our concerns incredibly trivial," he said finally.

Maggie looked astonished. "Oh no. Not at all.

"The carpets of snowdrops at Rochford Manor. Your lovely yellow Harriet. I've been to the Sudan. And the Congo. When you've seen…" she gestured.

"I would never consider the cultivation of such beauty trivial."

Thomas was about to reply when a gong sounded and Lady Ainswick announced, "Dinner is served. Would you please join us in the dining room."

There was no protocol observed as the group moved across the hall into the dining room, in which case Lord Raynham would have taken in Lady Ainswick and Lord Ainswick would have taken in, whom? Maggie had no idea. She'd have to ask Anne. Or check Debrett's, as her friend had suggested.

The dining room was another elegant room, painted a pale aqua. It had a ceiling plastered with garlands of fruit and flowers and was illuminated by more crystal chandeliers. A massive china cabinet that stood against one wall was filled with blue and white antique Chinese porcelain, while on the opposite wall more ancestral portraits hung.

Maggie checked the table and found there were no place cards that evening. Lady Ainswick sat at one end of the long, beautifully set table and Lord Ainswick at the other. Professor Wolford sat with Lady Ainswick and Violet and Sylvia quickly took places on each side of Lord Ainswick. The rest of the company sorted themselves as they came in.

Thomas took the chair beside Maggie.

"Shouldn't you sit with Lady Ainswick?" she asked quietly.

"Not tonight," he replied firmly. His blue eyes were warm and Maggie felt her cheeks get hot.

"Don't take this personally, Eliot. It's not like he'd want to sit with Sarah Pusey," she told herself sternly.

The meal started with potted shrimp, a dish that was not one of Maggie's favourites but was frequently served at dinner parties because of its popularity and simplicity; it could also be bought ready-made. But Maggie had not been able to develop a taste for the tiny creatures—how were their shells removed?—suspended in a crockery pot of melted butter that subsequently congealed under refrigeration.

The dish was to be eaten with toast, but, since British toast tended to be served at room temperature, the butter stayed congealed. Fortunately for Maggie, the starter was offset by some excellent white Burgundy from the Manor's cellar. Roast lamb followed, with potatoes, parsnips, carrots, peas and some equally first-rate Bordeaux.

"How do you find Oxford?" Thomas asked while they ate.

"Compared to the Harvard? The politics and faculty dynamics are similar and the students are equally bright. Oxford is rather tradition-heavy. I'm still not sure I've grasped all the finer points. It is quite glorious architecturally. The bells and spires. Even after eight years, it still moves me. On the other hand, the Boston metropolitan area offers resources a town like Oxford lacks. And I do miss being close to the ocean. A river just isn't the same."

"And you must miss your family."

"My family? Not so much. I'm afraid they don't really approve of me."

"Really? I would have thought they'd be proud. Your Great Aunt Margaret notwithstanding."

Maggie smiled ruefully. "Actually, Great Aunt Margaret was probably one person who would have approved. Or least understood. She taught Greek at a women's college. Otherwise, I think I was expected to make more… traditional choices."

She passed Thomas the wine and he noticed a signet ring on her right hand. Like her legs, Maggie's fingers were long and elegant. Maggie saw where he was looking.

"My father's. He was a cardiologist. And taught as well."

"Chief disapprover?"

"No, actually. My oldest brother became a neurosurgeon and that satisfied the need for footstep following. And filial one-upmanship. My father would have liked me to have gone to Harvard, though. This was his class ring. He was pleased when I got my Cambridge appointment. Our Cambridge, not yours. He gave this to me when I left for Oxford."

"If not Harvard, where did you study?"

"Great Aunt Margaret's women's college. Which some people say explains a lot. And then Yale."

"Does your father ever visit?"

Maggie shook her head. "He died a year ago Christmas. A heart attack. Ironic, considering."

Maggie sipped her Pommerol. "And you? Where did you study?"

"Balliol."

"And if you had not come into the title?"

"I studied military history. Can you see me as a professor, Professor?"

Maggie laughed. "I'll need to think about that one."

She paused and hoped Thomas would not regard this as intrusive. "What do you do when it's not snowdrop season?"

"Whilst I guess you could say snowdrops are our specialty, the gardens are in season pretty much year round. And there's the rest of the estate."

"The rest?"

"Sheep," said Thomas succinctly.

"Oh. I'm afraid I know even less about sheep than I do about snowdrops. Although after this weekend, I will certainly know more about snowdrops than I used to."

"Sheep have been raised at Beaumatin for centuries. The snowdrops are relatively recent in comparison."

"How do you feel about that?" asked Maggie curiously. "Your being, what, the 26th Baron? Do you feel like your life, what you do, has been pretty much, er, pre-ordained since you inherited?"

"In fact, I'm the 28th Baron," corrected Thomas. "I didn't become the heir until I was twenty and I didn't inherit until I was thirty-five, although by then I was spending all my time on the estate. How do I feel?" he considered. "I don't believe I've ever really thought about it."

Maggie was surprised by that, but didn't want to seem pushy by asking any more personal questions. She changed the subject.

"Do you get to London often? Or do the sheep keep you pretty much at home? I'm a big fan of the city. Oxford can get a bit suffocating at times and London for me is like coming up for air." She smiled at Thomas.

He smiled back and Maggie's heart did the fluttery thing. She realised that, unlike the previous evening, Thomas had completely ignored Daphne Townsend, who was seated on his left, while, it had to be said, she had not said a word to Damien, who was on her right and had been happily nattering away to Anne.

Something in Thomas' gaze turned speculative. Maggie broke eye contact and Thomas seemed to recall she had asked a question.

"London? No, not often. I blame it on being traumatised by a visit to the Tate Modern when it first opened."

"The Tate Modern? Quite understandable. Anne says a friend calls it the Stupid Tate, as opposed to the Proper Tate. I do like the Proper Tate, though. Especially the Pre-Raphaelites. Do you know them? Burne-Jones? Dante Gabriel Rossetti? I expect it's the hair." She gestured to her curls.

Thomas nodded slowly. "Yes, I know Rossetti. We have one of his paintings at Beaumatin."

"Really? It must be wonderful to be that proximate to such art. To have a… a daily relationship."

"You do get used to it. But I try not to take it for granted." He paused.

"I'd be happy to show you one day, if you like."

Maggie reminded herself that Thomas was just being polite and responded neutrally, "Thank you. That's very kind."

Chapter Ten. Magnet

Vigorous, healthy and a centenarian, 'Magnet' is characterised by Bishop, Davis and Grimshaw as "a mainstay for collectors around the world" and "defining a certain standard of garden worthiness." The sterile triploid should not be confused with 'Galatea'. 'Magnet' has a long, curved pedicel which carries the flower well out from the spathe and allows it to sway charmingly in the slightest breeze.

This iconic snowdrop was raised by James Allen and is thought to be a seedling of 'Melville Major'.

Dinner was served and cleared by two local women. There was no sign of Charlotte. Or, thankfully, of Edward. After coffee had been poured and whisky and brandy offered, Lady Ainswick stood and announced, "And now, let us have our auction."

She passed around sheets that listed the snowdrops to be offered, while one of the women who served the meal rolled in a cart with the snowdrops themselves, planted in small pots or "in the green," as Lady Ainswick called it. The second woman passed around bidding paddles like the ones used in prestigious auction houses.

"Chloe will be our auctioneer and she will set the opening bid price. The list is organised from the more readily available to the most rare. The last five are not yet offered on our sales list, so this is a special opportunity for you."

Maggie read through the selection, then asked Thomas, "What would you recommend?"

"For your friend? Does she already have a variety?"

"No. I think she only has the common nivalis."

"All right. You might try these." Thomas took out a pen from an inner jacket pocket and ticked half a dozen snowdrops that were in the first half of the list.

"And is there one of the more special varieties?"

Thomas considered. "You could try Deer Slot. Or perhaps Lapwing."

Chloe announced. "Our first snowdrop is S. Arnott. Bidding starts at £5.00, with bids of one pound increments."

Anne, Sarah, Graham and Derek all bid, with S Arnott finally going to Derek for £12.00.

"Our next snowdrop is Magnet. Bidding starts at £6.00, with bids of one pound increments."

The same group bid and Graham Townsend won Magnet for £15.00. He seemed surprised but pleased by his success and Daphne Townsend looked proud.

"Our next snowdrop is Art Nouveau. Bidding starts at £10.00, with bids of two pound increments."

This time the contenders were Anne and Sarah, with Daphne and Damien substituting for Graham and Derek. Anne got Art Nouveau for £22.00.

As the auction continued, Maggie noticed George Pusey tried to restrain Sarah's hand when she went to raise her paddle with a £28.00 bid. She angrily jerked her arm away

The Ainswick Orange

and raised the paddle defiantly. Maggie was glad Damien ended up with the winning bid of £36.00. Maggie managed to win three plants for Anne, but with over £100 pounds spent, she decided to enjoy being a spectator for the remaining items.

As Chloe worked her way down the list, Violet joined in and then Sylvia. The two women competed fiercely and finally it was just Violet, Sylvia and Damien bidding at prices Maggie found absurd, especially given what she knew about Violet's financial situation.

Bidding began on the last snowdrop to be auctioned and Maggie decided to try an experiment.

"Our final snowdrop offered this evening is Green Tear. Bidding starts at £50.00, with £10 pound increments."

Violet, Sylvia, Derek and even Anne began bidding. At £100.00, Anne dropped out. Derek folded at £120.00. Sylvia answered a bid of £150 and, when Violet failed to raise her paddle, Maggie raised hers. Sylvia quickly raised her bid to £170. Bid followed bid and Thomas murmured to Maggie, "What are you doing?"

Sylvia was breathing hard but Maggie remained calm. Then Sylvia raised her paddle for £390.00 and it was over.

"Yes!" she cried and pumped her arms in the air.

Lady Ainswick looked hard at Maggie and then nodded as though she understood. She announced, "Thank you for participating in our auction. Chloe will prepare your snowdrops and your receipts. You can claim your plants tomorrow at the Study House. I regret that Mr Mitchell is not here, but we will do our best to see he is suitably remembered."

The company stood to stretch their legs and enjoy final cups of coffee or an after dinner drink.

"What did you think you were doing on that last auction?" Thomas demanded.

Maggie smiled. "I wanted to see how far Sylvia would go to get something she wanted."

"Beyond all reason, apparently."

"Exactly."

"So you mean you were… do you really think she might have…"

"Do I think she killed Mitch? No. But she might have had someone else get her the Ainswick Orange."

"What you did was risky."

"Perhaps. A little. But worst case it was nothing I could not afford."

Thomas shook his head.

Sylvia was still crowing over her triumphs to Geoff and reviewing the list of her winnings. The rest of the group were saying their thank you's and good nights and gathering coats and handbags.

Thomas helped Maggie on with her jacket.

"It's a beautiful night. The moon is out and there's a short cut back to the inn via a footpath. Would you let me walk you back? Then you can use it when you come tomorrow morning. It seems such a short distance to drive."

Maggie both desperately wanted, and desperately did not want, to walk back to the inn with Thomas in the moonlight. She knew it was a really bad idea. If he were simply being chivalrous, as she strongly suspected, she would feel like a fool for having the feelings she did. And if it were for the reasons a man usually asked a woman to go walking in the moonlight, she was afraid she would end up acting like an even greater fool. But her brain refused to come up with an excuse that did not sound rude, so she said, "All right. Let me tell Anne."

When she told her friend Lord Raynham was going to show her a short cut back to the inn, Anne didn't roll her eyes or grin or make a snide remark. She simply said, "Fine. I'll meet you at breakfast at eight tomorrow."

Susan Alexander

Chapter Eleven. Green of Hearts

Heart-shaped green markings on the outer segments give 'Green of Hearts' its name. G. plicatus 'Trym', also known as 'Ace of Spades', is assumed to be one of its parents.

'Green of Hearts' is sometimes confused with 'Trumps'. However, the latter flowers earlier and is taller than this relatively short hybrid.

'Green of Hearts' was first noticed in 1997 in John Morley's garden at North Green.

Maggie and Thomas set off across the Rochford Manor lawn and came to a high stone wall with a door. Thomas opened the door and they passed through into a wood. Where there would normally have been undergrowth, carpets of snowdrops glowed in the moonlight beneath the trees.

Maggie stopped short. "Oh, how beautiful."

They continued on the path. The ground was uneven and, in her heels, Maggie walked unsteadily. Thomas took her arm.

They came out of the woods and the path ran through a field of winter-dead stalks. Ahead they could see the lights from the inn. Suddenly Thomas stopped, pulled Maggie to him and gently kissed her. When she did not protest or pull away, he kissed her again, with considerably more passion.

"Oh dear," thought Maggie.

They kissed twice more but then, reaching the limits of what two fully-clothed adults could accomplish by kissing in the midst of fields waist-high with dried weeds, Thomas put his arm around her and continued towards the inn.

The car park area was quiet and the rooms, dark. Maggie took her key out of her pocket and hesitated. Thomas moved her back against the door of her room and kissed her mouth, her temple, her cheek, her neck. He murmured in her ear, "May I come in?" and removed the key from her hand.

After that things became a bit blurred. They were in her room and Thomas removed the butterfly hairclip so her curls tumbled loose. Then suddenly her dress was lifted off in one motion and she was standing there in her black lace bra, thong, garter belt and stockings. She felt her cheeks get hot.

Thomas stared at her in surprise. Then he laughed.

"Maggie Eliot, you are one very unexpected woman." He fingered the garter belt. "Too bad the thong won't come off without removing this first."

Then they were in bed. Maggie hesitated.

"Thomas, I don't know. It's been a long time."

"For me as well. But they say it's like riding a bicycle. You don't forget. Let's hope they're right."

But Maggie was tense and awkward.

Thomas paused.

"Oh. I'm sorry." She began to pull away but he tightened his hold.

"Thomas, I…"

"Shh…" he put his finger to her lips.

"It's all right, Maggie. Just relax," he murmured. "Trust me."

Afterwards they lay together and talked quietly.

Thomas offered, "I'm sure you've heard I lost my wife—gossip is the daily currency of the Cotswolds and the world of horticulture is the same. Harriet died four years ago last November. Ovarian cancer. Asymptomatic. By the time they found out, it was too late. She was diagnosed in June and died five months later. After that things were bad for a long time. I barely held Beaumatin together. Then one day, about a year ago, the snowdrops were out and I seem to have healed. I still miss her, but life, well, life goes on, doesn't it?

"William, my oldest, lives nearby. He's a barrister. He has two children, a boy and a girl. James, our middle child, wanted to be a sailor from the age of four. He's now a Commodore in the Royal Navy. He still loves the sea, but his wife Victoria prefers him on dry land so he can come home at night, so he's based in London. They have two sons, one of whom is also mad to go to sea. And my youngest is Constance. She's an epidemiologist and works at the World Health Organisation in Geneva. She's engaged to a fellow doctor there who's from Sweden.

"And you, you never married?"

Maggie sighed. "Almost. Twice. Other academics. But the understanding was that, while I could have a career, I also had to take the shirts to the cleaners, the kid to cello lessons and the empty bottles left after a faculty party to recycling. Somehow what I had in mind was a more equal partnership. So I declined."

Thomas hugged her closer. "When I became the heir, I found the estate and the gardens were a full time job. More than full time. I guess you could say I work at home. Harriet worked beside me. She loved the gardens."

Maggie thought of Beaumatin's Harriet.

Thomas played with her curls. He nuzzled her neck, then did something which made Maggie gasp. He pulled her to him.

"Exactly like riding a bicycle. But much nicer," he said softly.

Maggie woke up feeling disoriented. She wasn't alone. An arm was wrapped around her and a hand cupped her breast. Thomas.

Thomas! She'd gone to bed with the baron. Oh my God.

The numbers on the bedside clock radio showed 2:50 and Maggie's Left and Right Brains started a discussion.

Her Left Brain said, "Maggie Eliot, you slut. You've had sex with a man you haven't even known for forty-eight hours. What were you thinking?"

Her Right Brain responded, "Yes, and it was wonderful. He's wonderful. And we're adults. And unmarried. And I don't have to worry about getting pregnant. So why not?"

Her Left Brain said, "Because he's a suspect in a murder. Two murders. Not to mention that you've become emotionally involved with him."

Her Right Brain rebutted. "I don't believe it. I am our intuitive half and I trust him. He wouldn't kill Mitch and what would he want with the Ainswick Orange anyway? He has hundreds of snowdrops. And the Ainswicks are his friends. It's not like he could add it to his collection."

L.B.: You don't know anything about him. Maybe he needs the money and is selling it on to another collector. That estate must cost a fortune to maintain. Maybe the inspector's right and he got into a fight with Mitch and took the snowdrop to make it look like it was another thief.

R.B.: There are far more likely suspects. Sylvia. Edward. Some unknown poacher.

L.B.: You're just impressed by the title and the estate and the whole Gilbert and Sullivan 'He is an Englishman' thing he's got going on.

R.B.: Am not!

L.B.: Are too!

R.B.: Am not!

L.B.: And the emotional involvement I mentioned?

R.B.: I'll get over it. Anne will doubtless give me another kitten. Or a puppy.

L.B.: And what do you think he thinks of you?

Maggie had no response to that. What did he think of her? A stranger. An American snowdrop tourist. No longer young. Never especially beautiful. Was she low hanging fruit? Safe because she was leaving in a few more hours? Was he exercising some sort of galanthophile droit de seigneur?

Thomas said, "Maggie? Are you all right?"

She gave the smallest shake of her head. He gathered her to him and rested his chin on her curls.

"Don't worry, my dear. We'll figure it out."

Some time later, Thomas fell back asleep, snoring softly. But Maggie lay awake for another hour.

Chapter Twelve. Pusey Green Tips

G. nivalis 'Pusey Green Tips' was first offered by the Giant Snowdrop Company in 1960, under the name G. nivalis flore pleno Green Tip.

The Giant Snowdrop Company was established in 1953 by Brigadier and Mrs Mathias at Hyde Lodge in Gloucestershire. Hyde Lodge was formerly owned by Walter Butt, who had acquired snowdrops from Colesbourne Park that included seedlings of what became the exceptional snowdrop 'S. Arnott'.

As the snowdrop is naturalised in the village of Pusey, in Oxfordshire, it has become known as 'Pusey Green Tips'. Described as a "messy double" with splashes of green on the tips of its outer segments, Pusey Green Tips has several look-alikes that include 'Hambutt's Orchard', 'Pewsey Green' and 'Wendover Green Tip'.

Maggie looked and saw that it was six o'clock. She really, really needed more sleep. Without more sleep, she knew she'd look like hell warmed over.

Thomas was up, trying to be quiet, putting on his clothes.

"I need to go home. Change. It would be indiscrete to appear in the same clothes I wore last night."

"And sartorially incorrect?"

He considered this. "Not if I had been to Church."

"Ah. Church. I'd forgotten it's Sunday. Heathenish me."

Thomas laughed and bent to kiss her.

"I'll be back at Rochford Manor around ten. There's a tour group coming to Beaumatin this afternoon and I need to make sure everything's in order."

He left and Maggie tried to go back to sleep. But that was a losing battle, so she got up, showered and dressed. She packed her few things. It was still only 7:10, but she was desperate for coffee. Maybe there was someone in the inn's kitchen.

She went to the main inn building and tried the door, but it was locked. Well, even though breakfast did not begin until eight on Sundays, there would surely be people about soon. After all, it took some time to cook up all that bacon and sausage.

She stood in the car park, indecisive. She was trying hard not to think about Thomas and the previous night, but was having the same success as someone who is told, "Don't think about an elephant." Of course an elephant immediately pops into one's mind.

She told herself, "Worst case, I had a magical night that I can remember in my twilight years. Assuming I can remember anything in my twilight years."

Maggie decided to see if she could find the shortcut to the Manor from the inn's end. Last night she had been too... involved in the moment to notice exactly where it came out. She thought it was in the space between the main inn building and the stable block where the guest rooms were. Maybe there was also a door to the kitchen around the back and she could find someone to get her some coffee. She really, really needed some coffee.

She had been right. There was the footpath. Good to know. Now to see if there were a kitchen door.

There was a collection of bins against the inn's back wall. The cool February temperature kept the smell to a minimum, but Maggie decided she wouldn't want to stand here on a hot day in August.

Then she saw the tip of a trainer protruding between two of the bins. She came closer. The trainer was attached to a leg. The leg was Sarah Pusey's.

Sarah was dead. She had been stabbed. Maggie knew she had been stabbed because a wood-handled knife was sticking out of her chest. It had been plunged in repeatedly and there was blood everywhere. It had soaked into her "Eat Your Heart Out" top and collected on the ground around her. The blood still glistened. This had just happened.

Maggie felt faint and the world spun. She grabbed at the nearest bin and bent over. When the earth stopped spinning, she took another look at the dead woman.

Sarah's eyes were open and had rolled back in her head. Gruesome. Unlike Mitch, her lips were pulled back in a terrified grimace. Her studded black handbag lay near the body. Maggie noticed a small notebook was sticking out of the top.

Without stopping to consider what she was doing, Maggie took a tissue out of her pocket and used it to put the notebook into her own purse.

She backed away and found the inn did indeed have a rear door. It was locked, so she pounded on it frantically.

"Open up! Open up!"

Mike Markham appeared in an apron, unshaven and looking half awake.

"What the hell?" he demanded irritably.

Maggie grabbed him by the arm and pulled him over to the bins.

"It's Sarah Pusey. She's been murdered," she pointed.

Mike turned ashen.

Having heard the noise, Holly Markham and the waitress had also come out the door. The young woman saw Sarah, screamed, then fainted. Holly knelt beside her and patted her cheek.

"We need to call the police," Maggie instructed Mike.

While Mike went to make the call. Maggie ran back and knocked quietly on Anne's door. When it opened, she said, "There's been another murder. Sarah Pusey. I found her out behind the inn. And I took this."

Maggie looked around but saw no one. She carefully handed Anne the notebook.

"Don't touch it. No fingerprints. Find someplace to hide it. The car. Your suitcase. It may tell us why she was murdered."

"Maggie, are you mad?"

"Please, Anne. The police will be here soon. I'm afraid…"

Maggie didn't know quite why she was afraid. Not that finding two corpses in twenty-four hours wouldn't give anyone the heebie-jeebies. This was gut instinct at work.

"I need to go back and be there when the police arrive. Oh and call Lady Ainswick and tell her what's happened."

Anne tsked in exasperation. "All right, all right. I'll be with you as soon as I…. So go. Go."

Maggie rushed back, thinking, "And if I don't get some coffee soon, I will kill someone myself."

She got back just as Mike was returning from calling the police. The waitress had come to and was sobbing. Holly Markham was trying to calm her.

Maggie explained, "I thought I was going to be sick, so I left. I didn't want to mess up the crime scene."

Mike nodded. "You look like you could use a brandy."

"No, thank you. But some coffee would be very much appreciated."

I'll get you some."

"Thank you. White. No sugar, please."

Maggie wanted to contact Thomas but had no idea how to get in touch with him. She had to assume Lady Ainswick would call him as soon as she had talked to Anne.

Mike returned with a large mug of coffee.

"Oh Mike, thanks so much."

Mike shook his head. "Terrible thing to happen. Not the kind of publicity we need. And right after that other murder. Do you think they're connected?"

"Yes."

Maggie could see Lady Ainswick rushing along the path through the field. Her hair was in disarray and her jacket was misbuttoned.

"Maggie! Anne called me. She said there's been another murder. Is it true?"

Maggie nodded. "Sarah Pusey."

"Anne said you found her."

Maggie pointed to where the trainer was visible. Then she gestured to her mug. "Coffee?"

"No, thank you."

Lady Ainswick turned to Mike. "But might I have some tea, please? Earl Grey, if you have it."

Mike went back inside. Lady Ainswick followed him. "Let's wait in the lounge."

They went through the kitchen where sausages were indeed grilling and reached the lounge. The women sat down in two wing back chairs.

"I'm afraid that dreadful Inspector Grey will be here any minute."

Lady Ainswick glanced at Maggie.

"I called Lord Raynham. He is on his way."

Maggie blushed but felt a tremendous sense of relief. Lady Ainswick watched her and nodded, like she had verified a hunch.

"He left his car parked at the Manor overnight," she explained.

Before Maggie could respond, Anne burst in.

"Lady Ainswick, I'm so glad you're here."

Mike returned with Lady Ainswick's tea. She thanked him and Anne asked if it were possible to have some coffee. Mike looked grumpy but went back to the kitchen.

"It's a terrible thing," Lady Ainswick said. Then she asked Maggie, "What did you see? Do you feel able to tell me?"

"I was looking for some coffee," Maggie explained. "The front door was locked so I went around to the back and I saw Sarah. Or one of her trainers. She had been stabbed in the chest. More than once. It looked like a kitchen knife. The blood hadn't dried. It was still dripping. So it must have just happened. That's all I know."

"I don't understand," mused Lady Ainswick.

"Now Mitch, it seems obvious his death is tied to the disappearance of the Ainswick Orange. Or someone wants it to look that way. And I can imagine any number of people might have wanted to kill that awful man. But Mrs Pusey? My mother would have called her a bit common, but why would anyone kill her?"

Maggie remembered what she had heard Sarah say on Friday night. And also that Sarah had been with her when she had overhead Sylvia and Geoff the day before. She wondered if the woman had heard as well and what she had made of it. Could this be related?

"And poor Mr Pusey. Has he been told?"

At that moment, George Pusey rushed in.

"Sheila?" he cried.

He grabbed Anne's arm. "What's happened to Sheila?"

He started to leave but the three women stood in his way. Mike returned and also helped hold the man back.

"You can't go out there," Mike said.

"Sheila again. What's that about?" Maggie wondered.

"Mr Pusey, I think you need to sit down," said Lady Ainswick.

When the man was seated, she explained, "I'm so sorry to tell you, but your wife is dead."

"Dead? Dead? What happened? What happened?"

Lady Ainswick put her hand on George Pusey's arm.

"I'm afraid she's been murdered, Mr Pusey."

"Murdered?" Pusey gaped.

"Do you know what she was doing out so early, Mr Pusey? Breakfast didn't start for another hour."

George thought, then exclaimed, "That stupid girl! I warned her! But she did it anyway!"

The three women looked at each other.

"What do you mean?" demanded Lady Ainswick.

George opened his mouth to speak, then closed it.

"Nope. No, I'm not saying another word. Not until I've talked to my solicitor. Now I've got to make a phone call."

He marched off to a far corner of the room and pulled out his mobile. He was soon talking and waving his free arm.

"Now what's that about?" asked Lady Ainswick.

Maggie wondered if she knew. But as she liked to remind her students, "No opinions without first having the facts." She needed to check out that notebook.

"Why don't we all wait outside," proposed Lady Ainswick. "It's mild and sunny and there are some tables. I assume we won't be able to have access to the inn or its grounds once the police arrive."

Pusey had finished his conversation. Lady Ainswick walked the man out the door, followed by Maggie and Anne, and led him to a picnic table set out for warm weather pints and smokers in all seasons.

Others in the group had now appeared and were expecting breakfast. Violet. The Townsends. Derek and Damien. Professor Wolford was staying at the Manor. There was no sign of Edward Symeon. Perhaps he had left. Or was sleeping in. And where was Sylvia?

Anne went over to tell the group the bad news. Maggie heard exclamations and some swearing. An old blue Land Rover pulled into the car park at too high a speed and skidded to an abrupt stop. The door opened and Thomas jumped out.

Maggie thought with surprise that she had never felt so glad to see someone in her life. Thomas spotted her and came over. He held out his arms and she walked into them. He hugged her and she felt tears start but blinked them away.

"I am not a lesser woman. Only a lesser woman would cry," Maggie admonished herself.

She became aware the car park had suddenly become silent.

"I'm all right," she murmured to Thomas and moved away.

She was right. The entire group was staring at her.

Lady Ainswick said to Thomas, "Thank you for coming. Sarah Pusey, if that's really her name, as apparently there's some doubt, has been murdered. Poor Maggie found her. Sarah Pusey. Behind the inn. Stabbed with a knife. It sounds like a game of Cluedo."

She sighed. "The police will have a field day. And as for the study weekend. Well, I suppose we shall have to offer everyone a refund."

At that moment, three police cars pulled in. Inspector Grey and Sergeant Hilliard emerged, followed by some police constables.

"Very déja vu," said Thomas, echoing Maggie's thoughts.

The inspector stomped straight over to where Lady Ainswick, Thomas and Maggie were standing.

"So now what? I understand there's been another murder."

He said it belligerently, as though it were a plot to interfere with his Sunday morning football previews.

Lady Ainswick said, "Sarah Pusey has been stabbed. Professor Eliot found her behind the inn."

The inspector barked at the constables, "Secure the scene!" He shooed them towards the inn and two of the constables raced off with rolls of police tape. He turned and glared at Maggie.

"So. Professor Eliot. You've found a body. Again. You seem to be making a habit of this."

Maggie felt Thomas tense and put a hand on his arm.

"I was looking for some coffee and found Mrs Pusey. She'd been stabbed. We called you."

"So you say."

Grey turned.

"Sergeant Hilliard," he barked. "Stay with them." He gestured to the trio.

"Constable Richards, stay with the rest of these people and make sure they don't wander off. Apparently galanthophilia is hazardous to your health."

At that moment, Sylvia Biddle-Pew emerged from her room. She strode over in a wildly printed blouse, tight orange pants and matching platform boots. Her mink jacket was draped over her shoulders.

"Goodness. The police? Again? What am I missing?"

Anne took her aside and explained.

"And now we'll have to spend another day sitting around waiting to be questioned? Bor-ring!"

Sylvia turned to Violet, "Come on, Vi. Maybe there's something on TV. A cooking show or something. Gotta love those Hairy Bikers."

She turned to Mike, "Any chance of room service?"

As the two women walked off, Sylvia called back to the inspector, "You know where to find us."

Maggie watched the inspector's face turn a dull red.

"Well done, Sylvia," she thought.

"Inspector," interposed Lady Ainswick. "You can't expect us to stand around out here while you, er, do your thing. I suggest we all go to the Study House at the Manor until you can join us there. You can use the same room for your interviews as you did yesterday."

Maggie worried about what Grey was about to say, but he restrained himself.

"Fine!" he snapped. "Richards, Hilliard, go with them."

He glared at another police constable. "Horwich, keep an eye on those women. Make sure they don't decide to go off on a shopping expedition!"

Grey strode off towards the inn.

Maggie and Lady Ainswick got into Thomas' car.

Maggie called to Anne, "Anne, come with us!"

Anne got in the back seat next to Lady Ainswick. She leaned forward and said, "Maggie? I couldn't think of a good place to hide 'it,' so I brought it with me. It's in my purse,"

"Really? That's great. Um, Thomas, Lady Ainswick, I, er, removed something from the crime scene this morning and gave it to Anne. I thought it might help us discover what's going on."

Thomas almost drove off the road. "Maggie, are you mad?"

"Let her explain, Thomas."

"It's a small notebook. It was in Sarah's, or Sheila's, handbag."

Thomas pulled up in front of the Manor and slammed to a stop.

"Maggie, this is obstructing a murder investigation. If the inspector finds out, you could be charged..."

"Thomas, let her finish."

"First, on the way to Beaumatin Friday, I heard George Pusey call Sarah, Sheila. He quickly corrected himself, but Sheila is not a likely nickname for Sarah, is it? Or if he did use Sheila as a nickname, why didn't he call her that all the time? And this morning, when he found out she was dead, he also called her Sheila."

"I heard him and wondered about that myself," added Lady Ainswick.

"And then his reaction was hardly that of a grief-stricken husband. He said, 'The stupid girl! I warned her but she did it anyway.' And he refused to say anything more and said he was going to call his solicitor.

"I don't think the Puseys are who they say they are. I certainly don't think that they're married, at least to each other. It's always struck me as strange, their being here. They are really out of place and from what I can see have no interest at all in growing snowdrops."

"Not PLU, as my mother would have said," agreed Lady Ainswick.

"PLU?" Maggie asked.

"People like us," explained Anne.

"And then, well, I need to tell you about what I overheard yesterday," Maggie continued.

Her companions stared at her and Thomas asked, "What did you overhear yesterday?"

"In the afternoon, during the break, before Geoff's lecture on yellow snowdrops. The Puseys and Violet Ashbury went out to smoke and I decided I needed some fresh air. When I came back, only Sarah was still there, finishing her cigarette. We were about to go in when someone out of sight, around the corner of the building, said, 'Well, you've got it, don't you? You haven't messed that up too?' Actually, she used another word, but you get the meaning.

"And who was it?" Lady Ainswick demanded.

"Sylvia."

"And to whom was she talking?"

Maggie hesitated. She really didn't want to mention her suspicions about Geoff. Not based on conjecture. So she said, "I'm not sure. Sylvia came around the corner by herself and I never clearly heard the person to whom she was speaking."

Thomas said, "And you think she was talking about the Ainswick Orange and what was messed up was the murder?"

"That is certainly one way of understanding it. Of course, it could have been about a lot of things."

"And so?"

"Sarah, or Sheila, heard it too. She pretended not to, but suppose she figured it out. And she let the person know. And got killed for it."

Thomas said, "That's rather speculative, Maggie."

But Lady Ainswick thought differently. "Give me the notebook, Anne. I'll keep it until we can take a look at it."

Maggie warned, "Be careful not to get your fingerprints on it."

"I know. Ainswick is a great fan of those CSI shows."

Lady Ainswick had just put the notebook into her jacket pocket when the police constable knocked on the car window.

Lady Ainswick opened the door and the PC, taken aback, helped her descend.

"Constable Richards, my companions and I are going to arrange to have refreshments brought to the Study House. Would you please make yourself useful and be sure the urn that is there for hot water is full and has been turned on? It's in the kitchen, which is behind the main room."

The constable was flustered. "Er, certainly my lady."

The viscountess smiled graciously at the young man, who raced off to undertake his quest.

"I just hope the inspector doesn't find out we've co-opted young Constable Richards," she added.

"Oh do come in. I was serious about refreshments. No one has had breakfast. Perhaps we can organise some fruit and toast."

They followed Lady Ainswick into the Manor. She and Anne went back towards the kitchen, but Thomas pulled Maggie aside. He pressed her against a wall.

"What you're doing is very risky. Please be careful," he said softly. "And tell me I haven't fallen in love with a crackpot."

He leaned against her and kissed her, a long, hungry kiss, and Maggie felt like her bones were liquefying and she was in danger of turning into a large puddle on the Ainswicks' marble floor. Then Thomas released her and followed after Lady Ainswick. Maggie just stood, too stunned to move.

"Compartmentalise, Eliot. It can wait. What he said can wait. For now, just go and see about that toast."

Maggie found Lady Ainswick in the Manor's kitchen, a large, bright room dominated by the inevitable Aga. The viscountess was putting loaves of bread into a shopping bag. Another bag was full of fruit. Apples, pears, oranges, grapes, kiwis, bananas. She pulled butter and marmalade and jam out of a large refrigerator and pointed to a massive toaster.

"Thomas, you take that. We'll bring the rest."

The quartet trooped across to the Study House. The others from the group, minus Sylvia and Violet, had already arrived, including George Pusey, who paced about and looked less bereaved than anxious.

Constable Richards was bringing out the urn from the kitchen. Tea bags, cups, sugar bowls, assorted spoons and the regrettable jar of instant coffee had already been set out by Charlotte.

"You can put the toaster on the table," Lady Ainswick instructed Thomas. "There's an outlet behind there somewhere. Charlotte, we'll need some small plates and some knives. People can make their own toast as they please. Oh yes, and some large bowls for the fruit."

Lady Ainswick could have commanded an army with aplomb, Maggie decided.

The viscountess said to Maggie, "I need to go back to the house and finish my toilet," she pronounced it the French way. "Which, as you can see, was interrupted. Also Professor Wolford is there and both he and Lord Ainswick will require some attention. But you should be fine here. When you and Mrs Brooks are done being interrogated by that unpleasant man, let me know. Thomas, come with me please. We need to talk."

They were at the door when Inspector Grey and Sergeant Hilliard appeared. "I am going back to the house, Inspector," Lady Ainswick announced.

"As you wish," said the inspector.

"But Lord Raynham, we'd prefer if you stayed here. We have some questions."

Thomas and Lady Ainswick exchanged looks. Then Thomas said, "Very well, Inspector."

The inspector sighed and said to his sergeant. "Here we go again."

"Very déja vu," said Thomas.

The inspector studied him. "You got that right," he said finally.

He turned to Hilliard, "That lady professor. She found the body. Give me a minute. Then bring her in first."

Susan Alexander

Chapter Thirteen. Kryptonite

In the Superman stories, Kryptonite is a radioactive element from Superman's home planet of Krypton. Exposure makes Superman weak and helpless. In the various media (film, TV, comics) which present the Superman story, Kryptonite is typically green.

G. elwesii 'Kryptonite' is characterised by the green tips of its outer segments and its completely green inner segments.

Anne asked Maggie, "Are you going to be all right? You could ask for a solicitor to be present."

"A solicitor? I don't think so. What I could use is some more coffee."

"Didn't get much sleep?" asked Anne innocently.

Maggie frowned at her friend.

"You're glowing. And there was that incident in the car park."

"Oh dear. Look, Anne. If I even start to think about that now I will have a complete mental meltdown. So later, please."

Then Sergeant Hilliard was standing there. "Professor Eliot? The inspector would like to see you."

A few moments later, Maggie was sitting in the wooden chair. Again. With his now habitual scowl, DI Grey could have been as aptly named "Grumpy" as the snowdrop.

"So Professor Eliot. Tell me what happened."

"About finding the body?"

"No, about the Man U-Man City game. Yes, about finding the body."

Maggie gave the inspector her death glare, then took a deep breath.

"Get a grip, Eliot," she told herself.

"I was awake early and I wanted some coffee. It was another hour before breakfast was served, but I hoped there might be someone around in the kitchen who could oblige me."

"Doesn't your room have a hot water heater to make coffee?"

"Instant. I wanted fully leaded."

The inspector looked uncomprehending.

"Proper brewed coffee."

Grey doodled on his pad.

"So you went to the inn."

"Yes. The front door was locked, so I went around the back to see if there were a kitchen door that might be open. There's a row of garbage bins along the inn's back wall and I saw the tip of a trainer sticking out between two of them. I came closer and I saw her."

"What did you do then?"

"I felt faint. I steadied myself on one of the bins and bent over until things stopped… spinning. I know I shouldn't have touched anything but if I hadn't, I was afraid I would have passed out.

"I banged on the kitchen door. Mike Markham, who's the chef and co-owner of the inn, came out of the kitchen. The waitress and Holly, Mike's wife, came out. The waitress fainted. Holly Markham tried to help her while Mike went to call you."

Maggie paused, then finished with, "And I got some coffee from Mike."

"First things first, you have your priorities?" Grey said sarcastically.

"It was after he called you."

"Humpf. And you didn't see anyone else in the area?"

"No. There was no one."

"How well did you know Mrs Pusey?"

"Not well at all. We only met on Friday and she was not… very sociable. She tended to keep to herself and not talk much to the rest of us. She did make a lot of phone calls."

"Did you hear what they were about?"

"No. She kept her voice down."

"And there was no one else around? You didn't see anyone inside or outside?"

"No." This was the second time he had asked that question.

"So you have no alibi?"

Maggie shrugged.

"What were Mrs Pusey's relations like with Mr Pusey?"

"It's hard to say. They weren't at all lovey-dovey or demonstrative. I heard him tell someone, I forget whom, before dinner last night that they'd been married about a year and he hoped they'd soon have a family. I got the impression that Sarah was not as keen on the idea as he was. And he was not enthusiastic about her bidding at the auction we had. Do you know about the auction?"

"You tell me."

"Part of the weekend's programme was an auction of some of the Rochford Manor snowdrops. The varieties ranged from some fairly common snowdrops to some that were relatively rare and pricey. George was unhappy when Sarah went on bidding after the price of one reached £28.00. I remember because he tried to stop her by holding down her hand, but she yanked it away and bid anyway. But I don't recall them being especially cross with each other afterward. It was just that one incident."

"Very well."

Maggie thought carefully, then decided there was no risk in revealing the information. "Um. There is one thing."

"Yes, Professor Eliot?"

"I'm not sure that woman was actually named Sarah Pusey."

"What do you mean?"

Maggie told him about hearing George Pusey call Sarah "Sheila" on the way to Beaumatin and this morning when he found out she was dead.

"And while Sheila might have been a pet name that he called her... Well, I only heard him use it those two times and when he said it in the van, he quickly corrected himself."

The inspector looked at his sergeant, who said, "I'll tell the forensic team to check her bag and her room and see if she has identification."

"And make sure Pusey is the next person I see," Grey ordered Hilliard.

The sergeant left and Grey said, "One last question. You're sure you didn't see anyone between the time you left your room and the time you discovered Mrs Pusey?"

Maggie looked at the inspector for a long moment. Then she said, "That is the third time you've asked me that, Detective Inspector Grey. And my answer remains the same. Are we done?"

"For now," he said. "But I'll need your fingerprints. For elimination purposes. From when you touched that bin."

One by one people were called in. Most of the interviews were brief. No one had much to say about Sarah Pusey and, except for Maggie, everyone had still been in his or her room when the body was discovered.

Sergeant Hilliard was circulating and getting permission to take fingerprints and search people's rooms for traces of blood. "It's standard procedure. For elimination purposes."

Maggie was not worried about blood. Her room was tidy and her bag was packed. But even a casual look at the bed sheets would reveal more about her night than she wanted known. However, refusing to allow a search would arouse even more suspicion on the inspector's part and surely they had all seen evidence of sexual activity before. So she agreed.

Maggie had finally capitulated and had some of the instant coffee. "Better than nothing," she told herself. Now she needed to use the WC. She went down the hall. Behind her, Sergeant Hilliard was returning from one of the inspector's errands. Again he failed to close the door of the interview room completely.

Maggie tried the door of the adjacent room and found it unlocked. It contained file cabinets and a bookcase full of botanical reference books and gardening magazines. If she left the door open a crack, she could just hear what was being said in the adjoining room.

The inspector was questioning Thomas.

"So Lord Raynham, where were you this morning?"

"I got a call from Lady Ainswick around 7:30, perhaps a bit before, asking me to meet her at the inn. She'd been notified about the murder. As Lord Ainswick has not been well, she said she would appreciate my coming for support."

"Lady Ainswick must have a high opinion of you."

"We have known each other since we were children."

"So you went?"

"I left almost immediately."

"What time?"

"I don't know. I didn't check. Probably within five minutes of receiving the call."

"And can anyone confirm this?"

The Ainswick Orange

"What do you mean?"

"The time that you left."

"I don't know. One of my staff may have seen me. A groundsman perhaps. Or my housekeeper. I'd have to ask."

"We'd prefer to do the asking, if you don't mind, Lord Raynham."

"As you wish."

"So you arrived at the inn when?"

"Around eight."

"You made good time."

"There had been another murder of someone attending the snowdrop weekend. Lady Ainswick was distressed. I came as quickly as I could."

"So you left your place around 7:30-7:40 and arrived at the Rochford Inn around eight, is that correct?"

"Yes."

"And what about before that?"

"Before I arrived at the inn?"

"Before you left Beaumatin."

"There is a tour party coming to visit our gardens this afternoon and I was checking that everything was in order."

"And when were you doing that?"

"From around seven."

"And did anyone see you."

"Again, I don't know. Perhaps one of my staff…"

"And before that?"

"Before what?"

"Before seven?"

"The usual. I washed. Shaved. Dressed."

"What time did you wake up, then?"

"Six o'clock. Perhaps a bit before."

Suddenly Maggie knew what the inspector was going to ask next.

"And where were you when you woke up, Lord Raynham?"

There was a long silence. Then Thomas said, "I don't see how this is relevant."

"I'll decide what's relevant and what isn't."

There was another silence.

"I'll ask you again. Where did you spend the night?"

"I'd rather not say."

"Because you spent the night with Professor Eliot? How was she? She seems like she might be pretty hot stuff. Beneath that prissy front she puts on."

Again there was a long silence.

Maggie thought, "Oh good grief, Thomas. Don't let him provoke you. Tell him. It doesn't matter if the inspector knows. Then he'll ask me to confirm what you said and it's over."

As Thomas remained silent, the inspector continued.

"Of course, you're not exactly a young stud. Think you made the grade? It was hard for me to tell from what she said. Although maybe you having a title and all would be the important bit when the professor tells her girlfriends back in Oxford about her little adventure, and not your expertise in the sack."

Maggie suddenly got in touch with her own capacity for murder. She had never felt such rage, not even when she found out about the Lying Bastard's wife. Surely Thomas would not believe she had said anything like that to the Inspector. Dear God, she hoped not. What would he think of her?

"Would it surprise you to know, Lord Raynham, that someone saw you leaving Professor Eliot's room and going back behind the inn around 6:15? Just about the time Sarah Pusey was murdered?"

Thomas said nothing.

"Why did you kill Sarah Pusey?"

"I didn't kill her. I'd hardly recognize the woman."

"You were at two dinners with her. Sat through some lectures. She visited your gardens."

"She was a bottle blonde. Around thirty. Maybe. I can't be sure of her eye colour or even her height."

There was a pause. It sounded like Grey may have been looking through his notes.

"Very well, Lord Raynham. If you can provide Sergeant Hilliard with a list of your staff who might have seen you at Beaumatin this morning, that's all. For now."

Maggie heard the inspector's chair creak, as though he were leaning forward, and his voice was venomous.

"But you know what I think? I think forty years ago you got away with murder. And now you think you can get away with it again. That you're protected by your fancy title and your big estate and your la-di-da friends. But you're not getting away with it this time, you po-faced bastard. I'm making it my mission to put you away for the rest of your life if it's the last thing I do."

There was the sound of a chair's being pushed back and Maggie heard footsteps going back down the hall. Thomas', she supposed. When it was quiet she peeked out from her hiding place, quietly closed the door and went into the WC. She felt sick.

She was shocked by Grey's apparent vendetta and the hatred she had heard in his voice. He was focussed on Thomas and ignoring who might have actually committed the two murders. She wanted to find Thomas and tell him not to let that awful man get to him.

Maggie also wanted to tell Thomas she had said nothing about him or their time together to Inspector Grey, but did not feel that she could. If he knew she had eavesdropped on his interview, it would confirm his fear that she was a "crackpot." An even greater fear was that he would have found the inspector's insinuations so offensive he would want nothing more to do with her.

Maggie felt like weeping and chanted to herself like a mantra, "You are not a lesser woman, you are not a lesser woman." It was because she was tired. And the shock of finding Sarah Pusey, or whoever she was. And the unexpectedness of the previous night. She might not be a lesser woman, but she certainly was not herself.

Maggie washed her hands and splashed cold water on her face and went back to the main room.

Anne had been looking for her anxiously. "Are you all right? You don't look well."

Maggie made a gesture and looked around. She did not see Thomas.

"Just tired," Maggie said finally.

Anne was about to speculate aloud about how she came to be so tired, but Maggie looked so unhappy she stopped herself.

"Can I get you some coffee?"

"If I drink any more of that coffee, I'll get ulcers. It's too acidic."

Violet came up. "Sylvia and I, we were summoned," she explained. "But I wanted to tell you personally what I told the inspector earlier. I was out for my first smoke of the morning. Because of the stupid policy the inn has of not smoking in your room. Just after six. And I saw Lord Raynham leaving your room. And going off behind the inn."

Maggie thought to herself, "He was taking the footpath back to Rochford Manor. To get his car."

"Anyhow I was curious. About how it feels to have gone to bed with a murderer," she smirked.

Maggie wanted to protest that Thomas was no murderer, but she remained silent and just stared back at Violet.

Annoyed not to have provoked a reaction, Violet added, "And I wanted to say it to you to your face. I'm not one of those people who go around behind other people's backs."

The woman smiled, but her eyes were hard and mean. She walked off.

"I'll bet," said Anne, who had been standing there through the whole thing.

Maggie turned to her friend. "He didn't do it. He was going back to Rochford Manor to get his car."

Anne squeezed her hand. "Of course he didn't."

"But Inspector Grey told Thomas that he knew he'd spent the night with me. And Thomas doesn't know it was Violet who saw him. He thinks I was the one who told Grey."

"Well, you would have just been giving the two of you an alibi."

"But Grey never asked me. And he told Thomas… He said awful things. Like that Thomas was too old to perform. That the only reason I went to bed with him was because of his title and the estate. That it was a story I could tell my girlfriends. And he made it seem like I had said it." Maggie sounded close to tears.

Anne looked shocked. "The police can make up things like that?"

Maggie nodded. "They do it all the time. It's not illegal."

"But surely Thomas wouldn't believe…"

"Why not? It's not like he knows me very well."

"So tell him."

"But then I'd also have to tell him I eavesdropped when he was being questioned. He already thinks I'm a flake for taking the notebook. This would just confirm it. He'd think it was as bad as those things the inspector said."

Anne looked like she wanted to argue but decided to keep quiet.

"And to make things worse, Grey seems convinced that Thomas did it. Both murders. Because of what happened with his brother."

Maggie told Anne the story of Charles Raynham's death.

"But they need proof, surely," Anne finally said.

"Sometimes just having a good story to tell the jury is enough to convict someone. It's not unknown for an innocent man to go to prison."

"Then we're back to finding out who really did do it, Professor Marple."

Maggie thought, then said to her friend. "Mitch's murder. Without any evidence linking it to one of us, it could have been anyone. But Sarah's? Or Sheila's? That couldn't have been random. It has to be connected to what happened to Mitch. And it has to be someone attending the seminar. Who else would Sarah go to meet behind the inn and let get that close at that hour? Certainly not a stranger.

"I wonder if she figured out who killed Mitch. Or who wanted the Ainswick Orange. And was blackmailing him. Or her. And that's what got her killed."

"So if we can figure out who killed Sarah, we'll know who killed Mitch."

"Or vice versa."

"We need to see that notebook."

"As soon as we can leave here."

Chapter Fourteen. Hercule

Hercule is the French form of the Roman Hercules, who in Greek mythology is the demigod Heracles, the son of Zeus. Hercules was known for his strength and his adventures, which culminated in the famous Twelve Labours of Hercules.

In mystery fiction, Hercule Poirot is the Belgian detective created by Agatha Christie.

The snowdrop G. elwesii 'Hercule' has exceptionally long outer segments and green chevrons on its inner segments.

Maggie was sitting at a small desk in what Lady Ainswick called the "Ladies' Parlour" at Rochford Manor. The viscountess used the pretty room as her personal office. The ceiling was festooned with plaster garlands and the walls had frescoes of shepherds and shepherdesses flirting as their sheep grazed nearby.

In front of her lay Sheila's notebook. Maggie carefully turned back the cover using a ruler and put two blown glass paperweights on the pages to hold it open. No way would that vile Inspector Grey find her fingerprints on the paper.

On the first page was written:

Sheila Finnerty

The Daily Post

While not one of its readers, Maggie knew *The Daily Post* was a tabloid, full of celebrity scandals, royal family gossip, fad diets and sports. She had seen it at newsstands and dismissed it as the embodiment of the sensationalising "opinions before facts" school of journalism.

Was Sheila Finnerty a reporter? Given the amount of publicity galanthomania was getting, it was certainly possible that Sheila was at the snowdrop weekend to gather material for a story. In fact, it would explain why someone as out of place as Sheila had come.

Maggie went in search of Anne and Lady Ainswick. She found them in the Manor's kitchen. Anne was doing some washing up and Lady Ainswick was stirring a large soup pot that was steaming on the Aga. Kat and Maus, the bichons frises, lay on the floor at her feet.

"Lady Ainswick, Anne, it seems Sarah's real name is Sheila Finnerty and that she was a reporter for *The Daily Post*. At least that is what she wrote in the notebook."

The two women looked at each other and grimaced.

"*The Daily Post*? That piece of rubbish?" said Anne.

"A reporter? Undercover to do an exposé on the snowdrop craze? On Rochford Manor?" Lady Ainswick was dismayed.

"Lady Ainswick?" Maggie continued. "Do you think you could go talk to George Pusey? I don't think he'd talk to Anne or me but he might talk to you. Could you ask him directly? Find out his part in this?"

Lady Ainswick smiled like a crocodile fixing on its prey.

"I will see what I can do. I'll go find him first thing after lunch."

Anne followed Maggie back to the Ladies' Parlour.

"So let's take a look," said Anne.

Maggie turned to the first page of notes.

RHS West. 14

RCHFD → GM

US RB SB? SP?

RB → GM

Dorchester

RHS 15

Lunch RB / GM

RCHFD Succession? Heir?

Ainswick Orange????

RB → GM Job?

Ainswick Orange → Job?

Maggie copied Sheila's notes onto a blank piece of paper and then carefully put the notebook to one side.

"At least I can read her hand writing," said Maggie.

"And I don't think it's a code. More like shorthand. Or abbreviations," Anne commented.

"But what does it mean?" Maggie said.

"Well, RHS. That's easy. The Royal Horticultural Society."

"And West. 14. Could that be an address?"

The women considered. Finally Anne said, "No. But I think I may know what it means. Is there an Internet connection here? I need a browser."

She went off to find Lady Ainswick.

A short time later, Anne returned with Lady Ainswick, who was carrying a sleek laptop.

"Here you are." She put the laptop on the desk and plugged it in.

"They have WiFi," Anne explained.

"Appearances to the contrary, we are quite up-to-date at Rochford Manor. We even have a Facebook page you can like and Ainswick has an HD TV and a Sky Box."

Anne opened a browser and typed Royal Horticultural Society into the search box. In a few moments she said, "Well, that was easy. I only hope everything is going to be this straightforward. RHS West. 14 is the Royal Horticultural Society Plant and Design Show at the Horticultural Halls in Westminster, which was on the 14th and 15th of February."

The Ainswick Orange

Lady Ainswick explained, "It's the major RHS show for snowdrops. We had a stand there and an elaborate exhibit. Geoff went down to man it. Chloe also helped out. It generates a lot in sales and interest in the gardens here."

"Then that's probably what RCHFD → GM means. Rochford Manor and Geoff Mortimer," Maggie stated.

"Then what's US RB SB? SP? stand for?"

The three women looked at each other, at a loss.

Lady Ainswick finally said, "Well perhaps a break will help. I've organised a late lunch. So please come and eat."

She led Maggie and Anne back into the kitchen, where places had been laid at a large table. Thomas was there.

Maggie's stomach did one of its little flip flops. She mentally crossed her fingers and walked over to him.

"How did it go with Inspector Grey's inquisition?" she asked.

Thomas just looked at her. Finally he said, "It was not pleasant."

"Inspector Grey is not a pleasant man," Anne remarked.

"Indeed," said Thomas.

Lady Ainswick came over holding steaming bowls of soup.

"Please sit down," she said. "We are eating en famille. No standing on ceremony. It's just the four of us. Chloe ate earlier with her father."

As Maggie was standing next to Thomas, he pulled out a chair for her. She smiled at him again and murmured, "Thank you," but got only a curt nod in reply.

After that, lunch was like a bad dream for Maggie. Thomas was aloof and avoided eye contact. She managed to consume a few spoonfuls of her soup, but left the bread and cheese and salad untouched. In passing the cheese to Thomas, her arm brushed against his and he pulled away, putting more space between them. It was like sitting next to a glacier.

Had he really taken what the inspector said seriously? Without even asking her? Did he think she would say such things about him? That she was like that? That that was what she thought?

Or was she just a one night's stand for him? She had already been prepared for that, but then why had he said what he had earlier? Maggie felt like she was going to be sick.

Charlotte came in. She was flustered.

"Aunt Beatrix. The police are here. They're asking to speak to Lord Raynham."

Conversation stopped.

"I had better see what they want, then," said Thomas.

"Please excuse me, Beatrix."

"I'm coming with you," responded Lady Ainswick.

Anne and Maggie also stood and the group went into the hall where Inspector Grey, Sergeant Hilliard and two constables were waiting. Lord Ainswick and Chloe had appeared from the drawing room.

"Detective Inspector?" demanded Lord Ainswick.

The Ainswick Orange

DI Grey was avoiding Lord Ainswick's eyes.

"Lord Raynham," he said. "We'd like you to come with us. We have some questions we want to ask you at headquarters. We believe you can be helpful to our inquiries."

"As you wish," responded Thomas without expression.

"I'll call William," said Lord Ainswick.

"Thank you," said Thomas.

He left without even a glance at Maggie. The front door closed and she heard the police cars driving off.

"Well!" said Lady Ainswick.

"Cedric, you'll call William?"

"Right away," he said and went into a room that looked like a library.

Lady Ainswick regarded Anne and Maggie. "As they say in hunting, best to get over heavy ground lightly. Meanwhile, we need to get to work."

Susan Alexander

Chapter Fifteen. Green Tear

A very rare snowdrop which broke a record when it sold on eBay for £360 in January 2012, G. nivalis 'Green Tear' was found in the Netherlands by Gert-Jan van der Kolk.

'Green Tear' can be compared to 'Virescens' with its even green inner segments, while broad outer segments with distinct green striping are considered to be an improvement over 'Virescens'. 'Green Tear' also blooms earlier, in mid-season

Maggie was helping Lady Ainswick wash up after their disrupted lunch by drying the dishes. But her hands were shaking and she dropped one of the china plates on the flagstone floor. Shards scattered everywhere and scared the dogs, who raced out of the kitchen.

"Oh! I'm so sorry, Lady Ainswick."

"It's only a plate, my dear. And please, I think it's time you called me Beatrix. Come. Sit down."

Beatrix took Maggie's arm and pulled out a chair for her. She sat down in an adjacent chair and waited.

Maggie rubbed her eyes and pushed back her hair. She took a shaky breath.

"What will he do to him?" Maggie finally asked.

"That unpleasant Inspector Grey? Put him in a nasty room. Badger him with questions. Try to wear him down, I expect. It's not like he'll be beaten or physically abused. This is Britain. And William, Thomas' son, will be there soon, I am sure. And William is very good at what he does."

"But how can they even think Thomas had anything to do with this? The inspector seems convinced."

Lady Ainswick sighed. "It's that business from years ago. His brother. Are you aware of what happened?"

"Yes, Thomas told me."

"It was terrible at the time. Such a tragic accident. And then to have some policeman decide to go on a crusade. It's the title. And the estate. I think he would have sent the whole family to the guillotine on principle if it had been possible."

"Did you know that it was Inspector's Grey's uncle who led that investigation? And that he inspired Grey to become a policeman?"

"Oh dear. So it's personal and the inspector feels he has a score to settle," said Beatrix.

"Are you worried?"

"No, not yet. It will be extremely disagreeable for poor Thomas, but they will have to release him. As far as I know, they have no hard evidence that points to anyone. It must be very frustrating for Inspector Grey."

She paused. "And how are you?"

"Me?"

"Yes. It's none of my business, of course, but at lunch I sensed…. a lovers' quarrel?"

Maggie blushed. "What you must think… Someone I had just met…"

THE AINSWICK ORANGE

Beatrix put her hand on Maggie's arm. "My dear, the first time I met Ainswick, I knew in five minutes that I wanted to marry him. And here we are, over forty years later. Sometimes it happens.

"Friday, after we returned from Beaumatin, Thomas called. He asked who you were. Asked to come to the dinner. He had come alive again. For the first time since Harriet got sick. It seemed he had also experienced what the French call a 'coup de foudre.'"

Maggie considered this, then raised her hands in a hopeless gesture. "This morning, when we were bringing the bread and toaster and stuff over to the Study Hall, he said... well, everything was fine. Then, suddenly, after he was interviewed, he won't speak to me. He won't even look at me.

"I... I happened to overhear the inspector questioning Thomas. The door was ajar. Like yesterday. Grey knew Thomas had spent the night with me. Violet Ashbury saw Thomas leaving this morning and told him.

"But Grey said horrible things. Like that Thomas was too old to, well, you can imagine. That I was only interested because Thomas had a title. And Grey made it sound like I had said it. And I'm afraid Thomas believed him. Without even asking..." On the verge of tears, Maggie stopped abruptly.

Beatrix sighed. "Men can be so stupid."

She patted Maggie's hand. "Don't worry. If it's simply a case of a misunderstanding. Let me see."

The women finished cleaning up. Anne returned from talking to her husband Laurence and extending Mary Meadows' cat sitting assignment for Maggie.

"Time to talk to George Pusey, I believe," said Beatrix.

"Do you think he'll tell you anything?" asked Anne.

"Don't worry," said Lady Ainswick. "He'll talk to me."

Anne and Maggie went back to the parlour and Maggie decided she would try not to think about Thomas, but concentrate on Sheila's notes.

"So let's see what we have to far."

Maggie filled in what they knew.

Royal Horticultural Society Westminster, 14 February

Rochford Manor → Geoff Mortimer

US RB SB? SP?

RB → Geoff Mortimer

Dorchester

Royal Horticultural Society, 15 February

Lunch RB / Geoff Mortimer

Rochford Manor Succession? Heir?

Ainswick Orange????

RB → Geoff Mortimer Job?

Ainswick Orange → Job?

"Rochford and Geoff Mortimer," said Anne.

"Yes. Geoff certainly appears frequently."

"So, US RB SP? SB?" said Anne.

"Well, US could mean the USA," ventured Maggie.

"And RB?"

"Could it be someone's initials?"

"Of course it could."

Anne went through a mental list of the weekend's attendees.

"But no one who is here. And if those are initials, then US could be Ulrich Schmidt or Uriah Scroggins or…"

"I get your point," Maggie interrupted. "But SP? SB? SBP is Sylvia Biddle Pew."

"And she is from the US," agreed Anne.

"So who is RB?"

"And what does RB arrow GM mean? And SP SB if they do mean SBP are only noted that one time. But RB also shows up on the 15th as well."

"Maybe we've been wrong and Sylvia wasn't involved in the theft. Maybe this RB person was and it had nothing to do with any of us who are here."

"Let's move on," said Anne. "Maybe there'll be something else that will give us a clue."

"There's not much," said Maggie doubtfully. "The Dorchester. And a heart."

"Think she had a crush on a hotel?"

"She didn't seem like the type who has crushes," said Maggie.

"And here's Rochford again. And the heir. That's the loathsome Edward. I can see why that would interest her."

Maggie looked at Anne questioningly.

"Well, if you're doing an article about the privileged classes paying fortunes for small white flowers while benefits are being gutted and teaching staff laid off, having a dissipated roué like Edward in the picture would be frosting on Sheila's journalistic cake," explained Anne.

"Oh dear. I can understand that," said Maggie.

"But how would she have found out?"

"Well, look. She found out about the Ainswick Orange. Maybe the same way?"

"And she found out in London. That's where Mitch heard about it too. Or said he did."

"Too bad there's no TM in her notes. Do you think US means Mitch? He was American."

"But so is Sylvia and there's that SB? SP?"

The women sighed.

"I had hoped we'd be better at this," said Maggie.

"Aha. You want to be Maggie-to-the-rescue, is that it?" teased Anne.

Maggie just shook her head.

While they were waiting for Lady Ainswick to return, Anne googled Sheila Finnerty and *The Daily Post*.

"Well, there are about a quarter of a million hits on Sheila Finnerty, but none seem to be connected to *The Daily Post*," announced Anne.

"Was she a newbie at the reporter stuff?"

"Or was it a fantasy, like her crush on the Dorchester?"

"And what is the relationship between the Ainswick Orange and a job?" Maggie wondered.

"Do you think it could mean a job as in a heist? Do you think she overheard the theft being planned in London? Do you think RB is the thief?"

"You know, you may have figured this out," admired Maggie.

"If Sheila had recognised the thief as the person she saw in London that would certainly explain her murder."

"But who could it be?"

"Well, we already know one person here was using an assumed name. Maybe someone else is as well."

Anne thought. "Okay. We can exclude you and me, as well as Derek and Damien, I've known them nearly five years now. Professor Wolford also has to be who he says he is. Lady Ainswick knows him. Sylvia? Could she be impersonating the real Sylvia Biddle-Pew?"

"That would be an expensive operation."

"Well, the Ainswick Orange is supposed to be worth a fortune. Spend money to make money?"

Maggie googled Sylvia Biddle-Pew.

There were many references to the woman in the Philadelphia society pages. With pictures. Of the same woman who was at the seminar.

"So Sylvia Biddle-Pew is in fact Sylvia Biddle-Pew," Anne stated the obvious.

The women thought.

"The Townsends?" said Anne.

"You know, at one point I thought, if I were one of Rochford's competitors in the snowdrop business and wanted to send a spy to get insider information, the Townsends would be exactly whom I'd use. They seem so harmless. And they really are the only true galanthophiles in our group, besides the Professor. And completely unlike Sheila, who was totally out of place from the beginning."

"That could also apply to Violet Ashbury, then. She is certainly the type to be a competitive gardener. I know these women. They're ruthless. And look at how she went to Inspector Grey about having seen Thomas."

Maggie sighed. "We seem to be expanding our suspect list, not narrowing it."

"Yes. It would have been so much easier if it had been Mitch," agreed Anne.

Lady Ainswick returned. She was looking pleased with herself.

"I spoke with George Pusey," she announced.

"And he really is George Pusey. He really lives in Birmingham and he really has a printing business.

"Sheila Finnerty is his cousin. His mother's sister's daughter. He said that she had been keen to be a reporter since she was a child and that she had decided to do an article on the snowdrop craze to show what she could do to land a job.

He said she's also always been good at… 'digging up dirt,' is how he put it. *The Daily Post* said if she could do an exposé, they would consider publishing it. But she had to pay her own expenses until they could see the article and judge for themselves.

"She decided she would fit in better if she came to Rochford Manor as part of a couple, so she enlisted George, who was not initially adverse to an all-expenses-paid weekend in the country. Apparently he's recently separated and his wife's name actually is Sarah.

"George knew Sheila had gone to London to see the RHS show and that she had discovered something there. When she came back to Birmingham she was very excited but wouldn't tell him why. She hinted there might be some dramatic happenings while they were here. It never occurred to George the events might be criminal.

"George thinks Sheila was not surprised when the Ainswick Orange was stolen. In fact, he thinks she was expecting it. What she was not expecting was a murder. He said that, after they were finally back at the inn before our dinner last night, she jumped up and down on the bed shouting, if you'll excuse me, 'Holy shit! Holy shit, George! What a story this is going to be. Because I know who did it!'"

"And George said that Sheila also told him, 'Not only am I going to clean up on this story, but that rich bitch can afford to pay me to keep her name out of it!'"

"George says he told Sheila that would be stupid and dangerous and that she should tell the police, but he doesn't think she did. Sheila could be very stubborn."

"So Sheila didn't tell the police what she knew. Did George?" asked Anne.

"I don't think so. I believe all he said was that Sheila was a reporter who was undercover to do a story on snowdrops and either found out something or someone thought she knew something. Either way, he was in the dark."

"Rich bitch, rich bitch," said Maggie.

"Anne, do you remember? That's how Sheila referred to Sylvia and Violet when we were going to Beaumatin in the van and they took off in Sylvia's Rolls. Do you think RB could stand for rich bitch?"

"And it's RB and then SB and SP. There are no VA's anywhere."

"And we know Sylvia was in London at the RHS show and met Geoff there."

"So let's see what that gives us."

Royal Horticultural Society Westminster, 14 February

Rochford Manor → Geoff Mortimer

US Rich Bitch Sylvia Biddle? Sylvia Pew?

Rich Bitch → Geoff Mortimer

Dorchester

Royal Horticultural Society, 15 February

Lunch Rich Bitch / Geoff Mortimer

Rochford Manor Succession? Heir?

Ainswick Orange????

Rich Bitch → Geoff Mortimer Job?

Ainswick Orange → Job?

"So Sheila's notes suggest that it's Sylvia who's behind the theft of the Ainswick Orange. And maybe she's the murderer as well. Lady Ainswick, we may have solved the crimes!" concluded Anne.

Lady Ainswick shook her head. "Perhaps. But remember, there's no proof. And George isn't talking and anything we repeat is considered hearsay, I believe."

Anne abruptly deflated.

Maggie added, "And although it would seem quite in character for Sylvia to arrange for the theft of the Ainswick Orange, I have never thought she would commit murder. I don't think she's the type that gets her hands dirty."

"So we're back to where we started," said Anne morosely.

"Not quite," said Lady Ainswick. "But I for one have had enough murder and mayhem for one day. I suggest we take a break and reconvene tomorrow morning. Perhaps things will be clearer with fresh eyes."

Susan Alexander

Chapter Sixteen. Heffalump

From the garden of Primrose Warburg at South Hayes, G. 'Heffalump' was named for her late husband, Dr Edmond F. Warburg, whose family nicknamed him after the fictional elephant in Winnie the Pooh.

The outer segments of this double are widely spaced and somewhat narrow, which showcase the tightly packed inner segments that flare slightly at the apex. The well-defined inner marking is plainly visible.

On the short drive back to the Rochford Inn, Maggie said to Anne, "You know, I'm not sure that we're being all that different than that odious Inspector Grey. We're really making a lot of assumptions. With absolutely no evidence.

"We've eliminated people based on our impressions of them. We're focusing on people because of our prejudices. Just like Grey is focusing on Thomas. We don't really know if the same person who killed Mitch killed Sheila. Or even if Mitch's murderer was the one who stole the Ainswick Orange.

"And who says Sheila got it right? George Pusey may have thought Sheila was good at 'digging up dirt,' but it's not like she was a seasoned investigative journalist. I think we need to start over. And we'll need a laptop."

Anne thought. "You're right, of course. So do we make a run back to your cottage?"

"Unless you know of a closer laptop that's available."

Anne shook her head. "None that I can think of. Mine is twice as far. Let's just hope Inspector Grey or one of his minions doesn't see us driving off and decide we're trying to escape."

As the inn's car park was still full of police cars and a SOCO van, Anne continued right on past and in twenty minutes was pulling up in front of Maggie's borrowed cottage.

"Want some real coffee?" Maggie asked. "The milk should even still be fresh."

"You bet."

While the coffee was brewing, Maggie checked on Bear, who sniffed her outstretched hand and then stalked off.

Maggie said, "I'm sorry, Bear."

She followed Bear upstairs and grabbed some clean clothes. It was hard to believe it had been less than three days since she had left the cottage on Friday, so much had happened. She felt like she had been gone for weeks.

Downstairs, she told Anne about her impression.

"Is this what you meant when you said it might help if I got away?"

Anne grimaced. "Well, I didn't mean discovering two dead bodies. Nor did I expect you'd have a romantic, er, liaison."

Maggie sighed. "You mean a one-night stand?"

Anne hugged her friend. "Talk about star-crossed lovers. But I'm sure things could still work out."

The Ainswick Orange

Maggie was incredulous.

"You're kidding, right? You know what Nietzsche said about hope only prolonging pain? It's much, much better for me to regard it as a casual encounter."

Anne sensed it had been anything but casual for Maggie, but she said, "Well, we'd better pack up that laptop before they send the hounds out after us."

Only a single police car and the SOCO van were still parked at the inn by the time they returned.

"Let's go see how well the free WiFi works. We can use my room," said Maggie.

Back in her room, Maggie found the bed had been stripped and her suitcase lay open on it. There was fingerprint dust on most of the room's surfaces.

She checked her suitcase.

"At least I don't think they took anything. I feel sorry for the Markhams and their staff, though. I wonder if all the rooms look like this."

"I'll go take a look at my room and let you know," said Anne.

"All right. I'll try to clean up some of this mess and see if I can get online."

Maggie had wiped up a lot of the powder and had managed to connect to the Internet by the time Anne returned.

"My room is all clean and made up. Looks like Grey had them do a special job on yours."

Maggie sighed. "Well, let's get started. How do you want to do this? Alphabetically?"

"That would mean starting with Violet Ashbury."

"Or the Ainswicks."

Anne looked shocked.

"I know. But as far as I'm concerned, you're the only one I absolutely know did not kill Mitch because we were together. I hope you think that that eliminates me as well. Beyond that, I remain neutral. And I'm including Edward with the Ainswicks," Maggie added.

"Edward. Right. How could I have forgotten?"

"Because we haven't seen him today?"

"You know, that's true. We haven't. And he shouldn't have been able to leave because we were all told to stick around yesterday. I wonder what he's up to."

"Trying to sell an orange snowdrop?"

"Have you checked eBay?"

"Maybe that's the first thing we should do."

But neither the Ainswick Orange nor another similar snowdrop was being auctioned on eBay.

"Well, it was worth checking. Back to the slog. And good thing I have my Oxford library ID, which provides access to almost every publication there is plus has legal databases."

Maggie googled Edward Symeon. Edward Richard Wallace Symeon was listed in Debrett's as the heir apparent to the current viscount. There were also some listings from the *Tatler* from ten to fifteen years before. The Ainswick family at the races. Edward looking young and handsome at some charity gala.

Another link was listed. It was an article in the magazine *British Homes* about expatriates on Cyprus. There were pictures of Edward Symeon's comfortable villa on the island and its garden. Maggie skimmed through the article but found no other reference to Edward.

Maggie searched to see if there were an English language news publication for expats on Cyprus. There was. It had a website but no search function. Maggie checked a few issues. Nothing about Edward that she could discover.

Lord and Lady Ainswick themselves? She doubted anything she could find on the Internet would be useful. Chloe Symeon? She knew she worked at the Royal Botanical Gardens at Kew, but could find no mention of her on the Kew website. She did not know her fiancé's name, although she understood he was a botanist and also worked at Kew. Googling Chloe found her engagement announcement, and her fiancé's name, which was David Osborne, as well as a few pictures of her at some charity events in London. Again, nothing that suggested any connection to the murders.

Going alphabetically, Violet Ashbury was next. Unlike Sheila Finnerty, the name Violet Ashbury brought up only one hit on Google and that was someone in Essex, not Chipping Norton. The town's website listed various community groups, but Violet wasn't mentioned there either. She tried Philip Ashbury. Apparently there was a Philip Ashbury who was big in Art Nouveau pewter teapots, but no one contemporary. Maggie sighed.

Anne, who was lounging on the bed reading the latest *Vogue*, heard her.

"Harder than you expected?"

Maggie told Anne about what she had seen and heard on Friday night. Violet and her ex. Damien and Derek. Daphne and Graham Townsend. Sheila/Sarah and George Pusey. Geoff and Sylvia Biddle-Pew.

"Poor Violet. Financial problems? That might make stealing a priceless snowdrop appealing. I could even see her bashing Mitch with a rock to get it. And stabbing a blackmailing Sheila? I can picture that even more easily than her clobbering Mitch. Finding a buyer for the Ainswick Orange? That's harder, unless she and Sylvia are in this together and I thought we liked Geoff for that."

"What about Damien and Derek, then. Derek was pretty distraught."

"Derek does tend to be a bit of a drama queen."

"And they only have each other for an alibi."

"Again, I can see them wanting to have their revenge on Mitch. But what about Sheila? She would hardly call either of them a 'rich bitch.'"

"True," agreed Maggie. "Do you know if they were at the RHS show?"

"No. Do you think that's relevant?"

"Well, that seems to be where the Ainswick Orange rumours started."

Maggie stretched.

"You know, I'm surprised to hear myself say this, but I actually begin to have some sympathy for that awful

THE AINSWICK ORANGE

Inspector Grey. No wonder he's focussed on Thomas. It's so much easier than having to slog through all this."

Anne stood up. "Well, all this slogging, as you call it, has made me hungry. How about some supper?"

"All right. I could use a break."

"There's a place called The Vicarage down the road. Want to give it a try?"

"Sure. Why not?"

Maggie was not really hungry, but knew she should try to eat something.

"And I'll tell the Markhams they should make up your bed and clean up the room while we're out."

The Vicarage was, as its name suggested, a renovated Victorian rectory with period furnishings, a blazing fire and a menu that specialised in locally sourced products.

Maggie and Anne walked in and immediately spotted two people they knew.

Derek and Damien had finished their dinner and were having coffee. They brought their cups over and sat down with the women.

"Well, this is a nice surprise," said Derek.

"Small world," said Damien.

"You haven't been arrested yet?" Derek teased Maggie.

"No. But they took Lord Raynham away to question him at police headquarters," said Anne.

"You're joking!" Damien was shocked.

"They think he's the murderer? Mitch's and Sheila's?" Derek was equally taken aback.

There was an awkward silence and Maggie noticed both men were trying hard to avoid making eye contact with her.

"It's because of his brother. Do you know about his brother?" Maggie finally said.

"No," they said together.

So Maggie told them the story of Charles Conyers's death and Grey's vendetta.

"But don't they need evidence? Is there any evidence?" Damien demanded.

"Not as far as any of us knows. There wasn't forty years ago and there doesn't seem to be any now either. It just seems like it's because of his title." Maggie was indignant.

"Well. And to think we were worried about being gay," said Damien.

"Good thing you're not Sir Damien Hawking," teased Derek.

"Only after we rack up a slew of golds at Chelsea and we make the Queen's honours list," said Damien.

"If anyone ever calls me Dame Derek, they're dead. Oops. I guess I shouldn't say that."

"Anyhow I'm glad we got to see you. That sergeant told us we could leave after lunch tomorrow. George Pusey as well. On account of we have businesses to run. And because we're nearby. And Violet gets to go back to Chipping Norton and the Townsends to Devon."

"We were all having drinks in the lounge when he came in with the good news. But they want Sylvia to stay until Wednesday. I guess they figure once she's back in the US, they won't be able to get any further information from her."

"And was she pissed off. Her flight leaves on Wednesday," said Damien.

"First class, of course." Derek did a fair imitation of the woman's throaty contralto.

"And she told Sergeant Hilliard that if she wasn't on that flight, they'd hear from her lawyers. That she was sick and tired of being cooped up in this dump. Meaning the Rochford Inn."

"The waitress heard her. I think she wanted to spit in Sylvia's vodka rocks."

"Oh, no. Excuse me. Grey Goose on the rocks." Derek imitated Sylvia again.

"Anyway, I would think this means you two will be free to go as well," Damien said.

"I'm sure we'll see you again soon in Burford," Derek said to Anne.

"And don't become a stranger, now," Damien said to Maggie.

The quartet air kissed and the men left.

Maggie toyed with some leek and potato soup while Anne enjoyed lamb. They compromised on wine and shared some rosé Sancerre.

"So do you think the guys are right and we can go tomorrow as well?"

"I expect so," Anne said.

"I'm surprised Sylvia Biddle-Pew hasn't brought in some high-powered solicitor before now."

"Arrogance?"

"Or, if you have nothing to hide, why would you need a solicitor?"

"There is that," agreed Anne.

Maggie sipped her wine.

"So I guess tomorrow is it. In terms of our trying to figure out what really happened."

Neither wanted to voice her concern about what this might mean for Thomas.

Anne eyed her friend.

"How are you doing?" she asked.

"As well as could be expected. I'm compartmentalising. But this time, please, no kitten. Or a puppy. Or even a hamster. Bear is more than enough."

Anne smiled. "All right. I promise. But don't you think…"

"No. No thinking. It was… an adventure. That's what you said I needed, right? So now I should be able to go back and turn out the book in a week. Or in two weeks at most. Or at least I hope so."

"And as for Thomas and Inspector Grey. Well, I guess we'll just have to hope that at some point someone notices that there needs to be some sort of proof before they can charge him. And Lady Ainswick said Thomas' son William is a really good barrister."

Anne ate her last bite of lamb.

"Pudding?" Maggie asked.

Anne sighed. "They're probably excellent here. And I can imagine the custard sauce, but no. Some coffee, though. I'm thinking we're going to have a late night."

"And it will balance out the rest of the Sancerre," Maggie added and reached for the bottle.

The women returned to Maggie's room at the Rochford Inn and Maggie resumed her research. She quickly learned two things about her fellow study weekend attendees that were noteworthy.

The first was her discovery of why Graham Townsend was worried about being recognised.

"Listen to this, Anne," Maggie said.

"Graham Townsend is, in fact, retired from a high-level job in the City. But it was because he was forced to resign in the aftermath of a major insider trading scandal. He wasn't directly implicated, but he had been the supervisor of the wrongdoers. So because he was the one ultimately responsible for his department's oversight, the firm forced him out.

"Townsend also had to pay a fine of nearly £400,000 to settle pending litigation and avoid a prolonged legal process."

"That's a lot of money, I wonder what impact that had on the Townsends' finances," Anne mused.

"The article doesn't say and I'm not sure how we could find out. I'm sure the police have the resources, but Grey is so focussed on Thomas, he probably won't look twice at the Townsends. They seem so innocuous."

Thinking about accessing financial information led Maggie to consider telephones.

"And it's not just people's financial information. I'll bet everyone has a mobile and it would be really interesting to know who called or texted whom and when."

"You're right. The police are always checking phone records on TV, anyway," Anne agreed.

Maggie sighed. "How did Miss Marple do it? Of course she lived in the days before text messages and Facebook pages." She went back to work.

Professor Wolford was another surprise. He had also retired from Cambridge under a cloud, after a male undergraduate had accused him of sexual harassment. However, the case was never adjudicated and the fact that Lady Ainswick held him in high esteem slowed any rush to judgement Maggie might have made. She had known colleagues put in similar situations when a student had been unhappy with a grade.

For herself, Maggie was already aware of how she appeared on Google. In addition to her academic references, and the reasonably objective Wikipedia listing, there was the liberal press that tended to simplify her positions and take her words out of context. *The Guardian* had even christened her "the Burqa Burner," with the implication that this was a bad thing.

Ironically, it had been her experience that someone like DI Grey would not hold that sobriquet against her. In fact, it might even improve his opinion of "the snooty professor."

Just to be thorough, Maggie did a search on Ty Mitchell. Mitch had had several write-ups in the *Hartford Courant*, the most recent just weeks ago when he was interviewed about galanthomania. Being Mitch, he was not shy about offering his opinions as facts and Maggie mentally shook her head.

He had also contributed a few articles on snowdrop cultivation and breeding to some gardening magazines. However, as he had told Maggie, his own nameless business had no web site or other web references. And he did not show up on Facebook or even LinkedIn.

Then Maggie found an article in the *Philadelphia Inquirer* about a meeting of the Delaware Valley Galanthus Society the previous autumn at which Mitch had been a speaker. The article included a picture of Mitch. Sitting beside him was Sylvia Biddle-Pew.

"Look at this, Anne," Maggie said excitedly. When she got no response she turned around. Anne had fallen asleep. Well, it was after midnight and it had been quite a day.

So Mitch and Sylvia knew each other. They had given no sign of it that she had seen. Were they hiding their relationship, whatever that was? And had it been through Sylvia Biddle-Pew that Mitch had learned about the Ainswick Orange? Was Mitch Sylvia's Plan B or had he been trying to get the rare snowdrop for himself?

Maggie wished there were a way she could find out if Mitch had been at the RHS show in London. There was nothing on the RHS website. Perhaps Lady Ainswick could ask Geoff if he had seen the man there. He would certainly stand out in a crowd with his height and demeanour. Although, like Sylvia Biddle-Pew, Geoff had not indicated he had ever met Mitch before.

Thinking of Geoff reminded Maggie she should also check him out. It seemed Geoff had studied Plant Sciences at Oxford. He had written numerous articles on snowdrops for the major British gardening magazines and was featured in newspaper articles about the garden at Rochford Manor.

On a hunch, Maggie googled the Delaware Valley Galanthus Society. It had a basic website and listed Sylvia Biddle-Pew as its Chairwoman. None of the other officers named were familiar. On an Events page, she discovered that Geoff had spoken at a meeting the year before Mitch. There was no picture, but it seemed obvious that he had met Sylvia Biddle-Pew even before she had come to the RHS show in London.

Geoff and Mitch, both connected to Sylvia Biddle-Pew. Perhaps Sheila had been right after all.

Finally, Maggie overcame her reluctance and googled Thomas. If only to shut up her Left Brain, which was continuing to make noise in the background.

There was the expected listing in Debrett's. Born 15 August 1951, Thomas Hugh Alardyce Conyers had become the 28th Baron Raynham in 1986. Wikipedia included an impressive list of the previous twenty-seven barons, beginning with the first baron in 1271. Thomas' heir apparent was his son William Rupert Evelyn Conyers, and the heir apparent's heir apparent was William's son Harry Alardyce James Conyers.

Maggie found announcements of the death of Thomas' wife, Harriet, and, in the Oxford online library's newspaper archives, even of the death of his brother Charles.

THE AINSWICK ORANGE

But unlike the Ainswicks, there was nothing in the *Tatler* or *Country Life* about the 28th Baron Raynham. In fact, there was such a dearth of information, she googled Beaumatin.

In contrast to many other noteworthy gardens, including Rochford Manor, Beaumatin did not have its own website. It did receive mention in over a dozen listings of important British gardens, but visits were "by appointment only."

There were photos of Beaumatin during the snowdrop season, of course, but also pictures taken later in the spring and summer, featuring wisteria, roses, rhododendrons and a majestic yellow magnolia tree. Maggie was impressed by the beauty of the gardens and regretted that she would never get to see them at another time of year.

It was 2 AM. Maggie changed into her nightgown and lay down beside her friend. But she remained awake for some time, wondering what to do with the information she had acquired.

She decided she would collect it in a file and pass it on to Lady Ainswick if it became necessary. She did not know if they had the concept of "reasonable doubt" in the UK, but certainly what she had learned should shift some of DI Grey's suspicions away from Thomas. Worst case, Thomas' attorney might find it useful.

"Unfortunately, as I am not a lesser woman, I cannot pretend that my research uncovered any new suggestions about who could have killed Mitch or Sheila or stolen the Ainswick Orange, although the fact that Sylvia knew both Mitch and Geoff previously is interesting," Maggie told herself as she tried to fall asleep.

"So it's back to Sheila's notebook in the morning. Which, as it is already morning, is going to be grim."

Susan Alexander

Chapter Seventeen. Tubby Merlin

A midseason cultivar, G. 'Tubby Merlin' is tolerant of a wide range of conditions. It increases rapidly to form large clumps and is what is known as a "good doer."

With a distinctive olive green ovary and solid, similarly-coloured inner markings, 'Tubby Merlin' often generates two scapes that hold their flowers out in splendid contrast with its nearly prostrate grey foliage.

'Tubby Merlin' was cultivated in the 1960's in the Gloucestershire garden of E. B. Anderson in Lower Slaughter.

Monday morning was unseasonably warm. It was warm enough, in fact, that Maggie decided a jacket was unnecessary and that she and Anne could walk rather than drive to the Manor to finish up their work on the notebook.

Anne was her usual bright and fresh self, but after a second night with little sleep, Maggie looked haggard and had circles under her eyes. Even after several cups of coffee, she felt exhausted.

Maggie told Anne what she had found out about Sylvia's knowing both Mitch and Geoff in the past. Anne was surprised, as she also had not seen any indication that Sylvia and Mitch knew each other. She could not remember them exchanging even two words or a meaningful glance.

"Do you think Sylvia came on to Mitch like she has to Geoff? And then it ended? That could explain why they'd ignore each other," Anne speculated.

"Yes. But then what does that do to our theory that it was Sylvia who told Mitch about the Ainswick Orange? As a kind of Plan B?"

"Oh." Anne deflated.

"And it's not like we can ask Mitch. Maybe we can ask Sylvia if she knew Mitch at some point and see how she reacts. Or maybe Lady Ainswick could.

"I should put together a list of things we'd like Lady Ainswick to find out. Whether Mitch was at the RHS show. Whether Geoff knew Mitch. Whether Sylvia would admit to knowing Mitch," Maggie said.

Her Left Brain added: And whether Thomas was at the RHS show. And where he heard about the Ainswick Orange.

R.B.: I think we've tasked Beatrix with enough questions.

L.B.: And maybe whether he'd ever met Sylvia Biddle-Pew before. If she pretended not to know Mitch, there may have been other people she was pretending not to know.

R.B.: As I said…

L.B.: Well, at least you won't need to pretend to have never met Thomas. It's not like you'll ever see him again. You won't be going to RHS shows or making snowdrop garden visits. And it's even more unlikely that he'll attend that conference on immigration at Stanford where you're speaking next autumn.

R.B.: Thank you for telling us something we already know.

The women turned back to Sheila's notebook. The single page of notes was all that the book contained but, at the end, half a dozen receipts had been carefully preserved between the last page of the notebook and its back cover.

The first receipt was for Sheila's entrance to the RHS show on 14 February. The next receipt had "Rochford Manor" printed across the top. It was also dated the 14th. Apparently Sheila had paid £9.00 for a snowdrop named 'Tubby Merlin' at the RHS Show. Geoff's signature was scrawled across the bottom.

A third receipt was for a taxi ride that went from Greycoat Street to the Dorchester Hotel, also on the 14th.

"Greycoat Street is where the RHS Halls are located," Anne said. "But the Dorchester? That doesn't sound like Sheila's kind of place."

"The Dorchester. Who did I hear mention the Dorchester? I'm sure someone did."

Maggie rubbed her forehead. Then she jumped up and said, "Yes! I know. It was Sylvia. When she was checking in at the Rochford Inn on Friday night. She said when she was in London, she always stayed at the Dorchester. And it's also in Sheila's notes. Dorchester, with a heart next to it."

"So what does that mean? That she thinks it would be nice to stay at the Dorchester?"

"Well, that's not where she stayed," said Maggie.

"Here's a receipt for a hotel near Victoria Station. Not five stars. Barely three. For three days, the 13th, 14th and 15th. The total would hardly buy you one night on Park Lane.

"And here's another receipt for a lunch on the 15th. At someplace called Rex Whistler."

Anne looked at the slip of paper. "Rex Whistler. I know that place. It's a restaurant in the Tate Britain, which is a short walk from the RHS Halls. It's really nice. Although it might also be a bit upmarket for our Sheila."

Lady Ainswick came in, followed by Kat and Maus.

"Good news. The police have released Thomas. He's back at Beaumatin," she announced.

She glanced quickly at Maggie, who was silent, then peered over at the receipt.

"Rex Whistler? Now where have I seen a chit like that recently?"

Lady Ainswick thought for a moment, then looked grim.

"I'll be right back."

A few minutes later she returned with a file folder. It was labelled, "RHS Winter 2012 Expenses GM." She opened the folder, which contained an expense report. She leafed through the receipts, found the one she was looking for and laid it on the desk.

It was also from Rex Whistler, for lunch for two on the 15th. For £87.90. Among the items noted were two Grey Goose vodkas on the rocks.

"Grey Goose on the rocks. Isn't that what Sylvia drinks?" asked Anne.

"May I?" asked Maggie.

Lady Ainswick handed her the folder and Maggie compared the two lunch receipts. Sheila's was marked Table 8 and Geoff's was marked Table 9.

The Ainswick Orange

Maggie pointed this out.

"Sheila was lucky. Usually you have to book well in advance at that place. And to get the table next to Sylvia and Geoff? She couldn't have counted on that," said Anne.

"I'm not sure it was all that lucky for Sheila, as it turned out," said Maggie.

Maggie returned to the Rochford Manor folder and pulled out two taxi receipts. The first was from Greycoat Street to the Dorchester on the 14th, which matched Sheila's. The second was a return trip from the Dorchester to Greycoat Street on the 15th. At seven o'clock the following morning.

She checked Sheila's more modest collection. Another taxi receipt. Also from the Dorchester to Greycoat Street. Also at seven o'clock in the morning.

"So Sheila was following Geoff and Sylvia Biddle-Pew. Unless Geoff was also staying at the Dorchester?" Maggie asked.

Lady Ainswick shook her head.

"There were hotels more convenient to Greycoat Street. And Geoff's expense allowance doesn't run to Park Lane."

"So it seems Geoff spent the night with Sylvia Biddle-Pew. I'm sorry, Lady Ainswick," said Anne.

"And I think I can take a guess at what was discussed at that lunch," added Maggie. She pointed to three lines in Sheila's notebook.

Ainswick Orange????

Rich Bitch → Geoff Mortimer Job?

Ainswick Orange → Job

Lady Ainswick slouched for just a moment.

"Geoff? But how could he? Geoff?"

Maggie thought, then said, "Perhaps it was Lord Ainswick's heart attack. And Geoff was worried about the future of Rochford Manor. And what would happen when Edward inherited. And as for Sylvia, well, I imagine she could be extremely seductive."

At that moment there was a commotion outside the room. The dogs started barking and raced out. Maggie heard a woman shriek. Lady Ainswick, followed by Maggie and Anne, rushed into the hall to see Charlotte crouched on the floor, holding her hand to her cheek.

Edward Symeon stood in the middle of the hall, waving a sheaf of papers, with Anne's London lawyer, was it Peaky? No, it was Peevey, grabbing at Edward's other arm and trying to calm him.

Edward was yelling. "You can't do this to me! You can't! You can't!"

Anne rushed to help Charlotte. Lord Ainswick came into the hall holding a newspaper, followed by Chloe and Geoff, who had a mug of tea in one hand.

"You always cared more for your bloody plants than me. Always!"

"Edward!" snapped Lord Ainswick. "That's enough!"

Edward snarled. He lunged at his father, but was restrained by Peevey. So he spat and hit the centre of the viscount's chest.

There was a shocked silence. Then Peevey suddenly gave Edward a brutal punch in the stomach and followed it up with an undercut to his jaw that knocked him to the floor, dazed. The dogs rushed up to sniff the prone figure and Kat licked Edward's face.

"I'm very sorry, Lord Ainswick. I hope you'll excuse me. I tried to stop him from coming here. And this seemed the only thing to do." Peevey straightened his tie and adjusted his cuffs.

"That's all right," said Lord Ainswick.

"I didn't know you were a pugilist, Simon. That's quite a right you have," he added admiringly.

"Thank you, Lord Ainswick, I appreciate your understanding. However, I think it would be better to get Edward out of here before he can cause any further uproar," said Simon Peevey.

The solicitor took a folder from a briefcase that had fallen near the door. He handed it to the older man. "Here it is. Signed. Witnessed. It will be all right now."

Simon turned to the plantsman. "Geoff, do you think you could give me a hand? Lord Ainswick, I will see that Edward is put on a plane back to Cyprus as soon as the police allow. Hopefully tomorrow."

Edward groaned. The two men grabbed Edward under his arms and dragged him out the door. Simon's Golf was parked in front of the house, its doors left open. They loaded the groggy Edward in and Simon drove off. Geoff came back inside.

Lord Ainswick looked at the others and barked, "Well, come into the library. You all may as well know what that regrettable scene was about. Especially you, Geoff."

The group filed into the large, book-filled room. Anne and Maggie took seats on a small sofa, while Geoff stood behind them. Lady Ainswick and Charlotte sat in two leather wing back chairs and Lord Ainswick leaned against a large carved desk. Chloe stood near her father and the dogs settled at his feet.

"That unfortunate display. I do apologize for my son. I trust for the last time."

Lord Ainswick opened the folder, looked at the papers inside, and then placed it behind him on the desk.

"Edward has told me repeatedly, as well as half of Gloucestershire it seems, that when he inherits at my death, the first thing he will do is bring in tractors and plough under every last snowdrop at Rochford Manor.

"While for some years I discounted this threat, there is nothing like a heart attack to inspire a man to confront his mortality. So with Peevey's help, Edward has had to choose between the gardens at Rochford Manor and continuing to receive his monthly remittance. Not surprisingly he chose the remittance. Charlotte, you and Emily will be taken care of. Chloe, you already know what provisions have been made for you.

"As for Rochford Manor, the gardens are to be turned into a charitable trust. That way, Geoff, you need have no worries about the future and you can even look forward to training a successor one day."

Geoff looked like he'd had a shock. The mug slipped from his hand and the hot liquid spilled over Maggie.

"Ah! Oh dear," said Maggie, jumping up.

"Oh. I'm so sorry. Excuse me. So sorry. Here, let me help."

Maggie and Anne had both grabbed tissues from their purses and were using them to soak up the tea from Maggie's sweater. Geoff had taken out a pocket handkerchief and was using it to mop up the liquid on the floor.

"I'm so sorry. Careless. It was a surprise, is all. The news. Good news, of course, but unexpected."

Susan Alexander

Chapter Eighteen. Wasp

'Wasp' has very long, narrow outer segments that give the appearance of wings, while the striped inner segments suggest the belly of its namesake. In a breeze, the outer segments do seem to move like a flying insect and are an arresting sight in a group.

The aptly named snowdrop was found by Veronica Cross during a visit to the former Backhouse garden at Sutton Court in Herefordshire in 1995.

Maggie needed to change her sweater, which was tea-stained and damp and sticky. Probably her bra as well. Apparently Geoff used a lot of sugar in his tea.

Maggie set off on the footpath back to the inn and tried not to think about the last time she had walked there. She was exhausted and wanted to go home. Not home to the cutesy cottage or home to Oxford. But home to Boston. Or maybe she could find a job in Australia. Or even New Zealand. She figured that would be about as far away from the Cotswolds as she could get. Did they have snowdrops in New Zealand? She didn't know, but she hoped not.

Left Brain: So. I warned you.

Right Brain: Yes, you did.

L.B.: Was it worth it?

R.B.: Ask me in a year. Or two. Or three.

L.B.: You are not as modern a woman as you think. You got emotionally involved. You never were good at casual sex.

R.B.: You always do enjoy stating the obvious. Besides, he said...

L.B.: We both remember what he said. But if he is this volatile, hot one minute, icy the next, you are much better off without...

R.B.: And this is supposed to make me feel better how, exactly?

L.B.: Point taken.

The path was uneven and Maggie kept her eyes on the ground so she didn't trip and make an even bigger fool of herself. As she came out of the woods, still looking down, a flash of white caught her eye. Something white... and orange.

There was a shallow ditch separating the footpath from the adjoining field. In the ditch she saw a green plastic flower pot. And the Ainswick Orange.

The snowdrop looked like it had been dropped. Or tossed. It had come out of the pot with dirt still clumped around the bulb and rootball and it looked bedraggled. The soil was dry and needed water. But it was indeed the Ainswick Orange, with its orange ovary and bright markings on the inner petals. Two people had died for it. Now she had it.

Maggie thought of picking up the snowdrop and running back with it to Rochford Manor, like a Galanthus EMT. But Geoff was still there and she was wary. Plus it was evidence. So she wrapped the ball of dirt in a handkerchief. Then she carefully detached one of the flowers with its stalk and left it beside the pot and put the handkerchief with its precious contents gently in her pocketbook.

As she bent over the pot, Maggie saw the corner of a plastic bag stuck in some dried weeds nearby. She looked around, found a length of branch that had broken off some shrub and poked at the sack. It opened enough to reveal a pair of blood-soaked Prada sneakers.

She called Anne.

"Anne, find Lady Ainswick. Be very discrete. Tell her I'm on the footpath that goes to the inn. She knows where it is. I've found the Ainswick Orange. And some other things."

"What? You found it?"

"Yes, but don't say anything. To anyone, but especially to Geoff. Just get Lady Ainswick and come."

Maggie had another idea.

"And bring Sheila's notebook. Just be careful not to touch it. And don't forget the receipts."

While Maggie waited, feeling very exposed, she thought about everything she knew concerning the Ainswick Orange and the murders. And she believed she finally understood all that had happened and why.

In less than five minutes, the women appeared.

"What is it?" asked Anne, slightly out of breath.

"Anne tells me you've found something, my dear," said Lady Ainswick.

"Yes. Is this the Ainswick Orange?" she asked.

Lady Ainswick knelt and gently touched the withered flower with the tip of a finger.

"Yes, it is," she sighed and stood.

"And look, there's also this." Maggie pointed to the bag with the bloody Pradas.

"Recognise these?" she asked Anne.

"Sylvia's Pradas!" Anne exclaimed.

Lady Ainswick looked at the two friends.

"Sylvia changed into them for the garden tour on Friday. We all saw her wearing them," Anne explained.

"Sylvia Biddle-Pew," said Lady Ainswick with contempt. "Not only a thief, but a murderess."

"We need to get the police here. But first, did you bring it?" Maggie turned to Anne.

Anne carefully removed Sheila's notebook from a pocket using a handkerchief.

"I thought we could leave the notebook here with these other things. We've always needed to turn it in to the authorities and this seems like a good opportunity. No one will be the wiser."

"But Sylvia knows she didn't take it."

"Yes, but I don't think the police will believe her when she denies that."

Lady Ainswick looked pleased at this thought.

"One other thing. Could you be the one to call the police and tell them you found these things? If Inspector Grey thinks this is my discovery, he'll probably accuse me of planting evidence and arrest me instead of Sylvia," Maggie concluded.

"That dreadful little man," said Lady Ainswick.

"And Anne, may I borrow your car? There's someone I need to go and see."

Anne was about to ask whom and then realised what a stupid question that was. She reached in her purse and handed Maggie the keys.

"Be careful. The third gear can stick," was all she said.

Susan Alexander

Chapter Nineteen. Icicle

Originally misidentified as G. 'Mighty Atom,' 'Icicle' is noteworthy for its short height and chubby flowers. The hooded apices of its outer segments are a rare feature. Inner segments show a pale green chevron.

Given its own name in 1999 prior to being listed by North Green Snowdrops, 'Icicle' can also be mistaken for 'Raveningham.'

Maggie found the gates at Beaumatin were open. That was good. She didn't know what she would have done if they had been closed.

She proceeded up the winding, tree-lined drive. Had it really only been three days ago that she had first been here?

She parked in front of the grand house, which seemed deserted. She got out, took her bag, and went in search of Thomas.

She finally found him in one of the farther gardens, on his knees with a trowel, at work in a bed of snowdrops. He looked up when he heard footsteps crunching on the gravel path and rose. When he saw who it was he did not smile and his eyes were cold.

Maggie felt sick but said, "It's over. We know who committed the murders and why. I imagine the police are making an arrest right now."

Thomas looked sceptical.

Maggie thought, "This is not going the way I'd planned."

She added, "Well, do you want to know or not?"

"Will it take a long time?"

"Does it matter? Don't you want to know?"

"Fine. All right. Come sit over here, then."

Thomas did a Duke of Edinburgh walk, hands behind his back, over to the far side of the garden and pointed to a bench. It was beneath an arch covered in wisteria vines as thick as Maggie's forearm. The vines were bare now, but Maggie imagined they would be glorious in a few months.

Maggie sat and waited for Thomas, who apparently preferred to stand.

"No good deed goes unpunished," she reminded herself.

"So Sarah Pusey's real name is, or was, Sheila Finnerty. She had aspirations to be a reporter for *The Daily Post*, which I'd assume you'd know is a popular tabloid, but perhaps you don't. Anyway, with all the publicity galanthomania has been getting, Sheila convinced them to let her do a story on spec on the galanthophile set. Full of aristos fiddling while Tottenham burns, the whole class warfare thing the tabloids go for.

"She did some research on snowdrops, found out about the study weekend at Rochford Manor and decided the Ainswicks were perfect subjects. She signed up for the weekend and convinced a cousin, whose name really is George Pusey and who actually lives in Birmingham and runs a printing business there, to pose as her husband.

"But first she went to the Royal Horticultural Society Winter Show in Westminster, where Rochford Manor had a stand. She met Geoff and bought a Tubby Merlin. Then she saw him with Sylvia Biddle-Pew, who had flown into town for the show, also before coming to Rochford Manor for the study weekend.

"Sheila thought Sylvia and Geoff seemed to be awfully chummy, which could be because Geoff had spoken at a snowdrop association meeting organised by Sylvia in Philadelphia the previous year. Curious, or suspicious, Sheila followed them back to the Dorchester, where Sylvia was staying. Geoff didn't come out until the following morning. George Pusey told Lady Ainswick that Sheila always was good at 'digging up dirt.'"

Maggie paused to see if Thomas had any reaction, but his face was unreadable.

"Go on," he said.

"Now we need to backtrack to the previous week, when Lord Ainswick had his heart problem. Geoff had heard Edward say numerous times over the years that the moment Daddy breathed his last, he was bringing tractors into the Manor and ploughing up every last snowdrop. Edward hates snowdrops with a passion, based on his conviction that the Ainswicks always cared more about their precious garden than him. But you know all this.

"Geoff saw Lord Ainswick's heart attack as the writing on the wall and believed that as soon as Lord Ainswick died, he was out of a job. So Geoff was of a mind to be open to potential opportunities. And in Sylvia Biddle-Pew, he saw a possibility.

"Our Sheila continued to track Geoff and Sylvia. At the RHS show on the second day, Geoff took Sylvia to lunch and Sheila managed to snag the table next to theirs. She overheard Geoff talking about his concerns regarding Edward and also about the Ainswick Orange.

"Sylvia became obsessed with getting it for herself and you've seen how Sylvia gets when she wants something. She told Geoff that if he got her the snowdrop, he had a job. Geoff agreed. After all, if Edward were going to destroy the gardens, why not take the Ainswick Orange?

"So it's the Snowdrop Study Weekend and Sylvia was expecting Geoff to steal the Ainswick Orange for her, as was Sheila. Why Geoff waited until then is not clear. Perhaps he thought the more people that were around, the more suspects there would be. And he may have been right about that.

"What he hadn't anticipated was that anyone else had heard about the snowdrop. We think maybe Sylvia had told Mitch about the Ainswick Orange, as a possible Plan B, in case Geoff didn't come through. We do know that Sylvia knew Mitch from the US. He had also spoken at Sylvia's snowdrop group, just last autumn.

"Anyway, however Mitch knew, both men went out to steal the Ainswick Orange on early Saturday morning when they thought no one else would be around. Whether Mitch followed Geoff or Geoff surprised Mitch, again we don't know. What we do know is that Geoff ended up killing Mitch and taking the snowdrop.

"But Sylvia was not happy about Mitch's murder and the attention it had called to the missing Ainswick Orange. Without the murder, it might have been days before the theft was discovered and she could have been safely back home with her trophy. That's why Sheila and I overheard her saying to Geoff, 'Well, you've got it, don't' you? You haven't messed that up too?'"

"It was Geoff she was talking to?"

"I think so. Sheila and I saw him almost immediately afterwards, coming around the other side of the Study House to make it look like he hadn't been the one with Sylvia."

"And you didn't mention this because…"

"Because, unlike Inspector Grey, who is happy to act without evidence, I had no real proof it was Geoff to whom she was talking. His appearance just then could have been a coincidence. And between the murder and the theft and Lord Ainswick's health problems and Edward's return, I didn't want to upset Lady Ainswick any further by suggesting her garden manager might be involved, based only on an assumption.

"Anyhow, even though Sheila pretended she hadn't heard Sylvia talking to Geoff, obviously she had, because she told Cousin George that she now knew without a doubt who had the stolen snowdrop. She didn't tell him the identity of the person but implied it was a woman—a 'Rich Bitch' as she called her—who would pay a lot to keep it a secret. And that she, Sheila, was going to have a talk with that person. George told her not to do it, that it was dangerous, but Sheila didn't listen.

"Sheila confronted Sylvia at the Ainswicks' dinner and arranged to meet her early Sunday and for her to hand over some cash. Only Sylvia surprised Sheila and stabbed her instead. Sylvia was also incredibly lucky in getting from her room to the meeting place and back without being seen. You would have just missed them. However, stabbing is a messy business and Sylvia's blood-soaked Prada sneakers have been found in a bag in the field behind the inn. As well as Sheila's notebook.

"So Sylvia is being arrested. While there's no hard evidence against Geoff as yet, I am sure Sylvia won't go down alone. And once Geoff knows Sylvia has turned on him, he should also be more forthcoming."

Maggie sighed. "What's so tragic, or perhaps ironic, about all this, is that it was all so unnecessary. Lord Ainswick's heart attack also made him think with more urgency about the future of Rochford Manor. And he gave Edward an ultimatum. Agree to give up the gardens or be cut off without a pence. Effective immediately.

"For all his awfulness, Edward isn't stupid and you can't hire tractors if you don't have any money. So he signed the papers this morning and now when Lord Ainswick dies, the gardens will become a charitable trust. Apparently the Ainswicks are providing for Charlotte and Emily as well. Did you know Emily is Edward's daughter? Evidently Edward's getting Charlotte pregnant and then abandoning her was the last straw for the Ainswicks."

"So that's it? Geoff killed Mitch and Sylvia killed Sarah who is actually Sheila? But where's the evidence? Or is this just Maggie Eliot, Ace Detective?"

Thomas was sardonic and Maggie had to struggle not to show how much he had hurt her. She stood.

"Some is from Sheila's notebook. And we have receipts from both Sheila and Geoff from London which match up. And the bloody sneakers. And Lady Ainswick had a talk with George."

Thomas said nothing, but Maggie could see the relief softening his face.

"A pity they haven't found the Ainswick Orange."

The Ainswick Orange

"About the Ainswick Orange..."

Maggie carefully removed the handkerchief from her handbag. She took Thomas' hand and placed it in it.

"This was with Sylvia's sneakers. It needs Galanthus intensive care, which I'm sure you can provide. I didn't want to leave it at Rochford Manor while Geoff was still there. It will be safer at Beaumatin for now."

Thomas cautiously opened the handkerchief and stared at the wilted flowers. Wilted, but definitely the Ainswick Orange. And the bulb seemed to be undamaged, that was the important thing. The rootball was also mostly intact.

He looked up to say something to Maggie, but she had gone.

Susan Alexander

Chapter Twenty. Hippolyta

In Greek mythology, Hippolyta is the Queen of the Amazons and the daughter of Ares, the God of War.

One of the Greatorex doubles resulting from a cross between G. nivalis flore pleno and G. plicatus, the snowdrop 'Hippolyta' is named after the Amazonian queen in Shakespeare's A Midsummer Night's Dream, whose approaching wedding to the hero Theseus forms the basis of the plot.

'Hippolyta' is one of the shortest Greatorex Galanthus. Its grey-green leaves are short as well. The double flowers are also distinguished by having very concave outer segments. The flowers hang elegantly from their long pedicels.

"So that's that," thought Maggie, as she drove back to Rochford. She and Anne would pack and, before she knew it, she would be back at the cottage. And if the events of the past days hadn't dented her writer's block, she didn't know what would. She would have to resort to hypnotherapy. Or exotic Asian herbs. With or without acupuncture.

Maggie felt frustrated that there was no real evidence against Geoff. Without hard proof, Mitch's murder would become a case of "he said, she said," and she believed that a British jury would not find Sylvia very credible. On the other hand, the woman could certainly afford the best legal talent.

Maggie thought back to Saturday morning. Finding the body. Anne going to get help. Waiting. Emily.

Emily.

Maggie could not recall anyone's talking to Emily. Grey had been so totally focussed on Thomas. But the child had been in the woods after the murder. Was it possible she had been there earlier? Could she have seen something?

Maggie got back to Rochford after only a few wrong turns. She drove past the inn, where police cars were still parked, and noticed some media vans with cameramen and reporters had arrived. She kept going and found the entrance to the Manor was thankfully clear. She parked the Range Rover, got out and went in search of the girl.

Looking more washed-out than ever and with a bruise on her cheek from having been struck by Edward, Charlotte was in the kitchen. She thought Maggie might find Emily in the woods having a tea party with her dolls. She didn't know exactly where. The child had several spots where she liked to play.

Maggie set off. She looked in the garden behind the house and the greenhouse, but didn't see the girl. Nor was Emily in the walled garden. Maggie took the now familiar tourist circuit but there was still no sign of Emily. One place remained to look.

Maggie found Emily in the dale, not twenty yards from where Mitch's body had lain and where police tape was still strung between the trees. She was sitting under a giant beech tree with three old-fashioned dolls dressed in cotton pinafores. On the ground in front of each doll, miniature china tea cups and small plates with a piece of a biscuit on each were laid out. Emily also held a tiny tea cup and was making polite conversation with her companions. She stopped when she saw Maggie.

Maggie smiled and said, "Hello, Emily. Do you remember me? I'm Maggie Eliot."

THE AINSWICK ORANGE

Emily nodded. She put down her cup, stood up and brushed some dirt and garden debris from her pants.

"Emily, do you remember on Saturday morning, there was an accident here and we talked?" Maggie gestured towards the crime scene.

Emily hung her head, but said, "Uh huh."

"Well, I was wondering. Were you also here before that? Maybe when the accident happened?"

Maggie held her breath and waited for a negative response. But Emily said nothing. She rubbed the toe of her trainer back and forth in the dirt. She drew one line. Then a second.

"Emily?"

Finally, Emily nodded.

Maggie asked very gently, "So you saw what happened?"

Emily nodded again.

"The big gentleman was looking for a snowdrop, Then someone hit him on the head with a rock. Do you know who that was? Did you recognize that person?"

Emily said nothing. She rubbed out the lines she had drawn with her foot.

"Emily, it's really important."

"Uncle Geoff," Emily whispered. "It was Uncle Geoff."

The two stood in silence. A breeze swayed the naked branches of the trees and a solitary bird sang an aria. Maggie hesitated, not sure what to do next. She turned around and nearly collided with Geoff Mortimer. He had approached without a sound.

"Oh!" said Maggie.

"Sorry," said Geoff.

There was a tense pause. Then Maggie said, "Anne and I are about to depart and I wanted to say goodbye to Emily. Charlotte said she was here, having a tea party." Maggie indicated the dolls and the china.

Geoff put his hand on Emily's head and stroked her hair.

"Yes, the grounds are a great place to play. I came to check out what damage the police had caused."

He looked over towards the crime scene. "Well, it could be worse, it seems. But I need to compile a casualty list for Lady Ainswick."

Geoff walked off and Maggie was left with a dilemma. She didn't want to leave Emily while Geoff was there, but she didn't want to arouse his suspicions either. She put her finger to her lips in the "Shh" sign.

Emily nodded.

"Take care, Emily," she said. Then added, "Goodbye, Geoff. I'm looking forward to returning when things are, er, less eventful."

Geoff had squatted down and was examining a plant that had been flattened. He waved.

Maggie felt she had no choice but to go back to the Manor.

Charlotte told her that Lady Ainswick had gone out on an errand. Mrs Brooks was at the inn, packing.

Maggie called her friend.

"Anne, it was Geoff! Emily Verney actually saw him kill Mitch!"

Maggie explained how she had been thinking about Emily's being in the woods and wondering if she might have seen anything.

"I had to leave her with Geoff, who is checking for snowdrop damage at Mitch's crime scene. There wasn't much else I could do. You don't think she's in any danger, do you?"

"I don't know. I just don't like it. Let's get Emily back to the house where we know she's safe." Anne sounded concerned.

In twenty minutes, Anne had reached the Manor. She had had to take the long way round to avoid the police and had been lucky to escape the notice of the reporters. Maggie was waiting in front of the house and they took off towards the dale.

There was no sign of either Emily or Geoff, but her dolls were still sitting in a circle and some enterprising ants had discovered the biscuits.

The women hurried back to the house. Lady Ainswick had just returned.

"Emily saw Geoff kill Mitch. Now we can't find her. Or him."

Lady Ainswick took the news of Geoff's guilt in stride.

"Perhaps she's with Charlotte," she said.

But the child was not with her mother, who was busy chopping some vegetables for soup in the kitchen.

"Very well," said Lady Ainswick. "You three go see if you can find her. I'll call that awful Inspector Grey. And please, be careful."

Charlotte took the path to the dale, while Anne decided to search the tourist trail. That left Maggie to look nearer to the house.

Emily was not in the formal garden or in the walled garden and the Study House was locked. However, on her way back to the house, Maggie noticed a light had been turned on in the greenhouse. Trying not to make any noise, she crept closer and peeked in.

Maggie saw that Geoff and Emily were inside. Emily was looking at some snowdrops, while Geoff stood at a counter that had a sink and the inevitable hot water heater for tea. He put what looked like several spoonfuls of cocoa in a mug, added a couple of spoonfuls of sugar and then, checking to make sure Emily was distracted, opened another tin. Maggie could just make out a large drawing of a rat and the skull and crossbones symbol for poison on the container.

Geoff put a heaping spoonful of white powder from the tin in with the cocoa. He mixed it and poured in some hot water and stirred. He took a marshmallow out of a bag lying nearby and ceremoniously placed it on top where it bobbled. Then he called Emily over and handed her the mug.

Maggie didn't wait to see what was going to happen next. She dashed around to the side of the greenhouse where the door was and burst in.

The Ainswick Orange

"Emily! There you are. Your mother wants to see you. Right away."

"Professor Eliot. I thought you had left," said Geoff warily.

"I was saying goodbye at the house and Charlotte came in, looking for Emily. It seems like it's important."

Emily took a big sip of her cocoa.

"Come with me, Emily. I'm sure Geoff won't mind if you take the cocoa with you."

When Emily took a second large sip, Maggie yanked the mug away and dumped the cocoa on the floor. She grabbed for Emily but the girl pulled away.

"Hey! Leggo!" Emily protested.

Maggie turned back towards Geoff and found him holding an ugly-looking knife he had snatched up from the potting bench. The blade was nicked and streaked with dirt. But it was long and the point looked sharp.

"I heard you, you know. I heard Emily tell you she saw me kill Mitchell," he said.

"And I told Lady Ainswick. So you might as well turn yourself in."

"I don't think so. Emily's a child. And a strange one at that. And if she accidentally mistakes some rat poison for sugar, well, that's tragic but no jury would believe what a dead girl reportedly said if I deny it. Without additional evidence. And there doesn't seem to be any, does there?"

"And Sylvia?"

"Her word against mine."

Geoff looked pained.

"She offered me a job, you know. In exchange for the Ainswick Orange. Put herself on offer, too. Said we had a future together. But I don't know. You women. You can't be trusted."

Maggie thought Geoff looked like he was about to come completely unglued. She moved directly between Geoff and the girl and yelled, "Emily, run! Get out!"

But Emily suddenly wailed, "I feel sick!" She bent over and vomited.

Geoff let out a cry in which rage, frustration and grief were mixed. He drew his arm back and lunged. Maggie tried to avoid the knife but was hampered by needing to keep between Geoff and Emily. The blade sank deep into her side.

"Ah!" Maggie had never experienced such pain. She doubled over and clasped her hands over the wound.

"I should have just told that asshole Mitchell to sod off. But I panicked. The rock was there. I didn't know about the trust."

Geoff's eyes filled with tears of self-pity.

"It's not fair!" Geoff wailed. He grabbed Maggie's hair to force her upright and struck again and again. He let go and Maggie sank down to her knees.

Geoff raised the knife and was about to bring it down once more when Maggie saw Lady Ainswick standing behind Geoff and holding a spade like it was a cricket bat. She swung it into the side of his head with a loud crack and Geoff collapsed.

"Emily. Poisoned. Can… counter," gasped Maggie.

Lady Ainswick bent down to where Emily was moaning on the floor, hands over her stomach. There was froth at the corners of her mouth and her legs twitched.

Lady Ainswick reached for a phone on the counter and hit a button. Someone answered at the other end.

"The greenhouse. Hurry. Call an ambulance and call the police."

Anne came running in, followed by Charlotte.

"Emily!" Charlotte cried.

Maggie collapsed and Anne caught her. She laid her friend on the floor, ripped off her jacket and pressed it to Maggie's wounds to try to stem the bleeding. There was blood everywhere.

From beyond Anne, Maggie thought she saw Thomas.

"Such blue eyes," she thought before everything went black.

Susan Alexander

Chapter Twenty-One. Miss Adventure

G. reginae-olgae subsp. veralis 'Miss Adventure' was first noticed by Matt Bishop on a visit to Anglesey Abbey in 1996. The gardens at Anglesey Abbey in Cambridgeshire are noted for producing snowdrops that include the eponymous Anglesey Abbey, Lode Star, Ailwyn and the unusual Anglesey Orange Tip.

Bishop was presented with a sample by Richard Ayres, who was the head gardener at the Abbey until 2001, and the plant flourished. The snowdrop features unmarked, paddle-shaped outer segments.

Maggie cautiously opened one eye. All she could see was white. "Am I dead?" she wondered.

She opened her other eye and tried to sit up, but failed. She noticed a number of tubes feeding into an intravenous drip in her right hand. She also had tubes of oxygen running into her nose. Additional tubes seemed to be coming and going from various other places.

Lady Ainswick appeared at her side. "How are you, my dear?" she asked.

Maggie had no idea how she was. Or where. Beatrix seemed to understand.

"You're in the hospital. In Cheltenham. Geoff attacked you. He stabbed you, but the doctor says he thinks you'll be all right. Eventually."

She paused. "That was yesterday. Today is Tuesday."

Maggie thought hard and remembered. The Ainswick Orange. The murders. Geoff's attack. She heard a sound and turned her head. A second patient was in a bed next to hers and Charlotte was sitting beside it.

"Emily?" Maggie croaked.

"She's going to be all right too. Thanks to you."

"Geoff?"

"Unfortunately, he's also going to be all right. He's in police custody. So is the Biddle-Pew woman. The evidence you found or, excuse me, that Anne and I found in the field was finally enough to convince Inspector Grey. As well as Geoff's attack. Even the inspector couldn't overlook that.

"And your friend Anne is here. She's gone to get some coffee. You know, you both should start attending Caffeine Addicts Anonymous," she smiled grimly.

Maggie moved her arm and it brushed her side. Oh, it hurt. It really hurt.

"You have a great number of stitches. You were in surgery for quite a few hours. You had lost a lot of blood. The knife made a gash in your stomach, penetrated your diaphragm and nicked a lung, in addition to cutting through a lot of muscle.

"Luckily Geoff is not very practiced at stabbing people and the knife deflected off some ribs before it could do any fatal damage. The knife was very dirty, so that has also been a complication. Whenever you need to manage the pain, just click this."

Lady Ainswick put a bulb on a long tube with a button at one end in her hand and clicked it a couple of times. Maggie felt herself drifting off, but managed to ask a final question.

"Thomas?"

"That man," said Lady Ainswick, "Is an idiot."

The next day Maggie's temperature spiked. She went in and out of consciousness, surrounded by doctors and nurses. She thought she heard Thomas yelling. But that was silly. Thomas didn't yell. It must be the morphine.

By Thursday the antibiotics were finally working and Maggie woke up to find herself surrounded by flowers. Lady Ainswick was sitting by her bed.

"You gave us a bit of a scare, you know," she said.

Maggie tried to smile and whispered, "Sorry."

"Do you want to hear the news?" Lady Ainswick offered.

Maggie nodded.

"All right. Let me know if you get tired. First, the police found Geoff's fingerprints on the inside of the flower pot you discovered that had held the Ainswick Orange. Thomas tells me it is doing well, by the way. Better than you are, in fact. They also searched Geoff's cottage and found a shirt with bits of, er, Mr Mitchell on it, hidden behind his kitchen sink. So there is finally some hard evidence.

"Confronted with the shirt, Geoff confessed. He said he was worried about his future at Rochford Manor. He had no idea Ainswick was setting up the trust. He was susceptible to Biddle-Pew, who offered him a job with, I think you'd call them benefits, in exchange for the Ainswick Orange. I guess spending a couple of nights with her finally persuaded him.

"We'll never know if the job offer was real or just something that woman promised to get him to steal the snowdrop. In any event, Geoff went out to steal the plant and came upon Mr Mitchell on the same errand. With his guilty conscience, Geoff panicked and killed him. He didn't stop to think he could have just thrown the man out and come back another time when no one was about.

"As for Sylvia Biddle-Pew, she admits that Sheila was trying to blackmail her over the Ainswick Orange. She claims that when she refused to pay, Sheila attacked her and her killing the poor woman was self-defence. She has an impressive legal team. I don't know what will happen.

"And speaking of people acting foolishly. Ainswick decided that if Inspector Grey had talked to Emily when you first mentioned you had seen her after the murder, and not been obsessed with his vendetta against Thomas, Sheila's murder, as well as the attacks on you and Emily, might have been prevented.

"So Ainswick talked to the Lord Lieutenant, who put him in touch with the Chief Constable, with whom he frequently works. The result is Inspector Grey has been re-assigned to Gloucester and put in charge of traffic control. And his side-kick, Sergeant Hilliard, has been sent to Cirencester in the hope that he can develop some independence of mind. And the Chief Constable went to Beaumatin himself to apologise to Thomas for Grey's behaviour."

Maggie nodded.

"Now I thought you might enjoy a tour of your flowers."

Maggie turned her head to see a veritable florist shop of blooms.

"The spring garden planter is from Fiske and Hawking." Daffodils fought with tulips, crocuses and hyacinths for dominance in the container. The scent of the hyacinths perfumed the room.

"The roses are from the Townsends, the orchid is from Mrs Ashbury and the mixed bouquet is from Anne and her husband. The Markhams sent the Siberian iris, Chloe got you the cyclamen and Professor Wolford came up with the pot of azaleas."

Maggie saw that left one small, delicate Limoges vase filled with a variety of snowdrops.

Beatrix sighed. "And the snowdrops are from Thomas."

Maggie waited.

"We have forbidden him the hospital. The doctors complained that the uproar he was causing was interfering with your recovery."

Susan Alexander

Chapter Twenty-Two. Comet

G. elwesii 'Comet' is known for being easy to grow and producing spectacularly large, shapely flowers that immediately attract the viewer. The flowers hang from long, graceful pedicels that extend from broad, glaucous, grey-green leaves. Some flowers display green markings at the end of the outer segments but this can vary from year-to-year. The inner segments have a broad, U-shaped mark.

'Comet' was first noticed by John Morley of North Green Snowdrops at Wisley in the early 1980's. With its long outer segments, 'Comet' is considered aptly named after the Kohutek comet of 1973.

A week later, Maggie was back at the cottage, having been pumped so full of intravenous antibiotics she felt like she must glow in the dark. She still had a side full of too many stitches to count and had been given bottles of more antibiotics and Percocet.

The doctor said he had done all that medical science could accomplish, the hospital needed her bed and she was to finish recuperating at home. She should come back in a few more days to have her stitches checked. Meanwhile, she was restricted to liquids like clear soup, herbal tea and apple juice. All at room temperature. And no coffee.

"Well, it's not like I can feel much worse," she thought.

Swallowing, breathing, moving, they all hurt. There was the Percocet, but Maggie hated the effects of the drug, which eased the pain but left her numb and apathetic.

However, as Anne had predicted, the break from routine had done wonders for Maggie's writer's block. Although she was only able to sit at her laptop for brief periods of time, Maggie had actually managed to generate the beginning of her first chapter.

What Anne had not predicted was the emotional devastation that was also the weekend's aftermath.

While Anne had urged Maggie to come and stay with her until she was fully recovered, Maggie had been insistent that what she most needed was some time alone.

"Bear will be company enough," Maggie assured her.

So Anne had reluctantly departed, with a promise to return every day until the stitches were out and with Maggie's pledge that she would call immediately if she needed anything.

What Maggie found she needed most were Kleenex. Except when she was writing or sleeping, Maggie was crying nearly non-stop. Her eyes were red, her nose was red and her upper lip was chapped from blowing her nose so much. There were boxes of tissues next to her laptop and on the table by the sofa. Damp used tissues were crumpled among her notes and journal articles. A waste basket full of wadded up Kleenex sat beside the sofa.

Maggie decided the tears were some sort of post-traumatic stress reaction. Or perhaps this was what the writer's block had been blocking. She refused to consider that they might be related in any way to Thomas. No. Not possible. Only a lesser woman would have had her heart broken after such a casual encounter. In any case, she hoped that the crying was therapeutic. It was certainly exhausting. And it hurt a lot as well.

She had just finished some further work on the book and was retreating to the sofa for a break when she heard tyres on the gravel in front of the cottage. Could it be Anne? Usually her friend would call if she were dropping by.

The lion's head knocker sounded on the door. Maggie sniffed and gave her nose a swipe with an almost-dry Kleenex. The knocker sounded again. She slowly crossed to the door and opened it.

Thomas was standing there, holding a large yellow hellebore in a pot.

"I thought you might be tired of snowdrops," he said. "May I come in?"

Maggie would have liked to say, "No. Go away, I never want to see you ever again," and slam the door in his face, but that kind of drama was not part of her repertoire. Plus it would not have been true. So she stepped back and gestured for him to enter.

Thomas looked at the long kimono of dark green silk brocade she was wearing. It had a fiery dragon embroidered down the length of its back. Bravado on her part, he decided. Maggie looked wan and exhausted and had obviously lost weight. It also seemed like she had been crying.

"How are you?" he asked with some concern.

"All right. I'm all right. I'm fine."

He gestured at the laptop and the stacks of notes and books and journals surrounding it.

"So I gather you've broken through your writer's block?"

"Apparently."

He set the hellebore down on the table, which startled Bear, who took one look at the visitor and raced upstairs.

"That's Bear. She's shy."

Thomas indicated the field of tissues. "Allergies?"

"Exactly. Allergies."

"Maggie, I…"

"Would you like some tea or coffee?"

Maggie was surprised to realise she didn't know which beverage he drank. How could she have become so besotted with someone and not even know if he preferred tea or coffee?

"No. Thank you."

There was an awkward pause.

Maggie gestured to the room. "So this is my Cotswold fantasy cottage. Charming, isn't it? Quaint as well. But be careful. The beams are low. I almost knocked myself out once going into the kitchen."

"Maggie, I... Please. Listen to me."

He took her hand and she froze.

"Maggie, please. I've been an idiot."

"Yes?"

"Yes. And Beatrix has also been telling me I've been an idiot, continuously, since, since I last saw you."

"You needed Lady Ainswick to tell you that?"

"Maggie, I'm sorry. I'm so sorry."

"Was it some gallant notion that you had to reject me because you were going to be arrested for murder?"

"No."

"Did you think I suspected you?"

"No."

"Was I too easy? Did I jump into bed with you too fast?"

He was taken aback. "No!"

"Then what?"

He hesitated, then came out with, "You told the inspector we'd spent the night together."

"What?"

"Beatrix says you were only trying to give me an alibi and it was foolish to mind."

"But I didn't."

"You didn't what?"

"Tell him. Because he never asked me. And I certainly wasn't going to volunteer the information."

"It wasn't you? You really didn't tell him?"

Maggie sighed. "No. I really didn't tell him. Anything. It simply never came up."

"Then how did he find out?"

Seeing Thomas still seemed confused, she expanded.

"Look. Everyone in the group had seen we were close and anyone could have mentioned it. Violet Ashbury said that she'd seen you coming out of my room that morning and that she'd told the inspector. Or someone else could have seen you. Or Grey could have just made it up to get at you. Policemen do that all the time."

Thomas was stunned. "I never thought of that. I really have been an idiot."

"Yes, you've said that. But why did it bother you? And if it did bother you, why didn't you just ask me about it, instead of…" Maggie was going to say "freezing me out," but decided not to.

Then she decided she really wasn't feeling fine at all and needed to sit down.

"Maggie?"

She had gone white.

"Maggie?" She waved her arm to keep him at a distance and walked unsteadily to the sofa. She tried to sit down carefully, but even so her stitches pulled and she inhaled sharply at the pain from her internal injuries.

Thomas followed her. "Maggie, what can I do? Can I get you something?"

She shook her head, with her eyes closed, and waved her arm again in a negative gesture. He caught her hand and held it and sat down beside her. He waited until she opened her eyes and took a deep breath.

"After Harriet died, I thought I'd never find another woman I'd care for, who would make me feel again like, like... and then I met you. And we had that night together. And you seemed to return my feelings. It was like a miracle.

"Then when the inspector brought it up, he made it sound so cheap. And tawdry. He said things... And I just assumed that, that it hadn't been the same for you."

Maggie felt the tears coming again. Phooey. She turned away and sniffed.

"Maggie?"

Maggie wiped the back of her hand across her eyes.

"Allergies again?" Thomas asked.

Maggie looked around for the box of Kleenex.

Thomas took a white cotton handkerchief out of his pocket and put it in her hand. Then he carefully took her in his arms while she sobbed. And he held her until her sobbing stopped. And then he kissed her.

"Oh no," Maggie protested. "I'm a total mess."

"Not to me."

"Lord Raynham, you are a hopeless romantic."

"I am? I'm not the one who wears black lace garter belts."

They sat together quietly. Thomas was still holding her and Maggie felt like she had come home, if home were a feeling and not a place.

"When I saw you in the greenhouse, there was so much blood. I was terrified you were going to die. That I was going to lose the only other woman I'd ever care for."

"That really was you? I thought I was seeing things."

"I'd come over to tell Beatrix about the Ainswick Orange. I assumed you had left."

"That was the plan, but on the way back from Beaumatin, I remembered that Emily had been in the woods when we discovered Mitch. And that no one had talked to her. Inspector Grey was so obsessed with trying to prove that you were the guilty one...

"I wondered if she might have been there earlier. And it turned out she had actually seen Geoff kill Mitch."

"Beatrix says you saved Emily's life. That you put yourself between her and Geoff. That it was an act of remarkable courage and self-sacrifice."

Maggie shook her head. "Reflex. No thought was involved."

Thomas gently gathered her closer.

"Come back with me to Beaumatin. You can't be having an easy time of it here on your own. You can recuperate there."

Maggie was about to decline, but he kissed her before she could say no. The kiss was neither gentle nor short and all she could do was wonder how she could feel so happy and be in so much pain at the same time. Thomas inadvertently tightened his hold and she cried out.

"Maggie! I'm sorry..."

She covered his lips with her fingers.

"I think we've had enough sorries."

"Then you'll come?"

"Thomas, you're very kind. But there's my work. And the cat. And I can barely manage the short flight of stairs here. And the idea of having to travel anywhere on these roads…"

"So you won't let me play your knight in shining armour and effect a very belated rescue?"

"Did I mention that you are a hopeless romantic?"

He smiled. Then he became serious. "Professor Margaret Spence Eliot. I've been here only a few minutes and it is obvious even to an idiot such as I that you are in no condition to be alone. So in addition to having to worry about your being a crackpot, do I also have to worry that you're pig-headed?"

"I am not a crackpot! And I'm not pig-headed."

"Prove it."

Maggie hesitated.

"Good. That's settled then. I'll stay here. I brought some things with me, in case I couldn't convince you to come to Beaumatin."

Maggie looked stricken. "But Thomas, isn't this your high season? You have visitors and, and…"

"Don't worry. I will be at Beaumatin when needed."

Maggie sighed. The man seemed to be determined.

"Did you know I can cook? I have quite a repertoire. Fried eggs. Scrambled eggs. Omelettes even. Toasted cheese sandwiches. Bacon. Sausages. Mash. Shepherd's pie. And I am a master at opening soup in a can and can heat anything that Waitrose offers ready-made. But no potted shrimp. You needn't worry about that. I could tell the other night you were not a fan."

"Oh dear. Was it obvious?"

"Well, it was to me. Now what can I do for you?"

Maggie gestured. "At the moment I'm only allowed clear liquids. At room temperature. There're some herbal teas in the kitchen. A cup..."

"Your wish is my command." He stood up and started towards the kitchen.

"Oh, Thomas? I'm afraid the cooker's an Aga."

"I expected it would be," he replied calmly.

"Oh. All right." Pause.

"Mind your head on the doorframe," she warned.

"And... By the way. Thomas?"

"Yes, my dear?"

Slightly taken aback, Maggie asked, "Do you prefer tea or coffee?"

"Why, coffee. Can't live without it."

Maggie had to smile. Perhaps there was a chance this was going to work out after all.

The Ainswick Orange

SUSAN ALEXANDER

About the author

A native New Yorker, Susan Alexander lives in Luxembourg, where she writes and undertakes research on public policy and the social sciences.

She is interested in writing about women who have lived complex and interesting lives and the choices they have made.